Y0-AUX-204

THE RED DIRT PARADOX

Gary D. Henry

Copyright © 2013 by Gary D. Henry

Library of Congress Control Number: PENDING

http://www.garydhenry.com
Email: virginian44@comcast.net
Facebook: Gary D. Henry
Twitter: @Gary Henry
Cover Design: Colleen Lockard
Cover photo: Seenu Baradwaja
Edited by: Mary Harris

All rights reserved. Except for appropriate use in critical reviews or works of scholarship, the reproduction, transmission, or use of this work in any form or by any electronic, mechanical, or other means now known or hereafter invented, including photocopying, recording, or by any information storage and retrieval system is forbidden without written permission of the author or publisher.

This is a work of fiction. Names, characters, places, and incidents either are the product of the author's imagination or are used fictitiously, and any resemblance to any actual persons, living or dead, events, or locales is entirely coincidental

DEDICATION

As always, dedicated to my family and friends. Live your life to the fullest. Create a wealth of memories in your lifetime, and relive them as often as you can because memories will be your riches when your allotted time on this earth has expended. Reflection will be our last greatest moment. Also dedicated to my sister, Belinda Bell, who tirelessly edited this book and others. She left us too soon.

Acknowledgment

I'd like to thank everyone associated with the creation of this book. Mary Harris for editing expertise and Colleen Lockard for her great cover and Seenu Baradwaja for allowing me to use his photo for the cover. I'd also like to thank Aileen Aroma for her encouragement and her marketing expertise.

Chapter 1
Remembrances

The year was 2011 and eighteen-year-old Trent Pritchard contemplated his life in a rural town named Red Dirt in the mountains of West Virginia. He was not a vengeful man even though life, as an adult, tested his limits. He was a simple man who just wanted to get through life unscathed and desired nothing more than what was in front of him. He grew up too fast because life thrust pain and unimaginable horrors on him at a very young age. Red Dirt was located just west of Lost River. A community so small that it really didn't have a name for most of its history, but the townspeople affectionately called it Red Dirt because of the deep red hue of it's fertile soil that appeared to stick to many a boot dirtying living rooms and businesses around town, and the name stuck.

The town consisted of one school, a small grocery market, a church, a bar, and his father Ben's, Sportsmen and Outfitters store, all surrounded by some of the most beautiful scenery in the country.

The store was also his home; his father built a three-bedroom house in the back, so his father's aching knees wouldn't have to make the trip every day to open the store in the wee hours of the morning.

Young Trent grew up curious about their little town and its history, and constantly asked questions about the people within it. His main source of the answers to his questions was his father, Ben. A respected member of the community, Ben was born and raised in Red Dirt and many felt that he was the resident historical scholar of the tiny town.

Ben saved newspapers, birth and death records, as well as many historical artifacts with regard to the small community's creation. Not minding the questions, Ben felt pride in Trent wanting to know about his heritage, and he happily answered his son's questions when asked. In addition, Ben loved talking about his youth and his life to that point: the hunting store; the time he met his wife, Trent's mother, Margie and growing up in the beautiful mountainous territory surrounding the town. His adventurous tales always drifted to hunting and fishing and stories of how big the bucks he bagged were, and the oft told story of his twenty-pound bass he caught at his favorite fishing hole.

Growing up in poverty in the town, had its hardships with regard to jobs and a constant lack of pocket money, but Ben and his close friends never complained.

They were kids whose parents taught them to care more about the land and what it offered.

***

Bagging his first deer at ten years old, Ben proudly displayed all his trophies on the walls of the rustic store, though none matched the trophy quality bucks his grandfather bagged during many hunting excursions.

Nonetheless, his father proudly and prominently displayed them among the much larger bucks he'd hunted in his later years.

The store wasn't always busy, so it provided ample opportunities for father-and-son discussions. Ben tried to shield Trent from many of the trials of living in a town that didn't keep up with technology and the attitudes of the outside world. He was thankful that the tiny town moved along at a snail's pace because it allowed his young son to grow to appreciate what they had. His father ensured that Trent had more than he'd had, even though Ben grew up as the town took root in post-World War II America and when the town's leaders created laws within the community.

Up to his eighteenth year, young Trent didn't really see that much hardship, as his parents' store provided for his upbringing.

When times and money were lean, a quick hunting trip brought home enough food for the family until sales picked up.

An intelligent boy, Trent sailed through school with perfect scores.

The old schoolhouse consisted of a single room with one teacher who was, unexplainably to Trent, an expert on every subject.

Growing up in Red Dirt, she hadn't gone to college; she'd learned what she knew from books she read. There was no subject where Trent struggled; however, if he had a question, his teacher or his father always had the correct answer to impart to him.

Ben and Margie hated the fact that they lacked the money to send him to college because his grades and enthusiasm seemed to scream higher education. It was a failing on their part that captured their thoughts on more than one occasion.

They made multiple attempts to save their money but, in the end, it proved never to be enough. The skyrocketing cost of a college education prevented many in the community from extending their children's education.

Trent read through some old books that his mother owned as a child and wanted to read them all, but not until after he'd stocked the shelves, swept the floors, and completed other tasks around the shop. The chores at the store took precedence over fictional stories of fanciful characters in impossible situations.

Ben possessed so much material about the town's history that he set up a corner of his store as a library of sorts and placed all the information on shelves with a table and a few chairs for his customers to sit down and read up about their family's history.

Trent and his father stocked the shelves with mementos from his father's past and historic newspapers that depicted important events in Red Dirt's history. Trent noticed an old book that interested him; as he thumbed through it, a photo fell from it to the floor. He placed the book back on the shelf, climbed down the small ladder, and picked up the photo. The old yellowed photograph depicted his mother and father and a few other individuals whom he didn't recognize.

"Dad, who are the kids in this picture?" He handed the photo to Ben.

"That's me, Randolph Kolb, Patch, Remy, Jordy Penchant and your mother. I think we were about nine years old. Where did you find it?" He handed the photo back to Trent.

"It was in a book on the shelf."

One boy in the photo piqued his interest. "Kolb? You were friends with Randolph Kolb?"

"Yes, he was in our circle of friends back then. Randolph is a lot different now than he was then. We were very close friends and, to me, he was my best friend. Something corrupted him along the line.

I think he's still around here and as you probably know, his boys have turned into a redneck terrorist outfit. I haven't seen that picture in ages," Ben lamented, as he continued to add books and photographs to his small remembrance corner.

Ben saw that the old photo created questions in his inquisitive teenage son. He didn't mind talking about his past, even though his past was painful at times and not as ideal as Trent's upbringing.

Trent resumed his gaze at the photo and recognized a few of Ben's childhood friends after his father told him who they were. "I know that Remy is the pastor and Jordy died a few years ago, but who's Patch?" He pointed to the smallish disheveled young man wearing a homemade leather floppy hat, similar to Trent's that he'd found on one of his hunting trips, in the photo.

"He used to be a dear friend of mine. He saved my life about a year after that photo was taken. I nearly drowned and he jumped in and saved me. I couldn't swim at the time and got my foot caught on something under the water and he got me out. It makes me happy that you're interested in these old photos," he stated with pride.

"I love all this old stuff, Dad. Where is Patch now?" Trent inquired.

"I don't know, but I returned the favor a few years later. He got lost in the woods for two weeks. The townspeople and his parents were frantic looking for him, but I knew where he went. I found him in the meadow up on the mountain, you know, that place I took you when you killed your first buck. I went there and found him. He'd nearly died up there. He hadn't eaten in weeks and too weak to walk any farther, so I carried him most of the way. I think that there is a newspaper article about it somewhere. A mountain lion just about got us but I fired off a couple shots and it ran away. It's easy to get lost in the wilderness if you don't know where you are; it can be very dangerous."

"What happened to him after that?"

"His parents and his three sisters died in a fire about a year after I carried him back, so my parents took him in. I think he was twelve or thirteen at the time. I went to his wedding after your mother and I got married but I haven't seen him since. He married a woman from New Jersey and I think he moved there."

"Did he ever come back here?"

"No. I think he and Kolb had some interactions but I have no clue what transpired," he explained, as he continued hanging nostalgic photos on the wall.

Trent dutifully worked at the store, stocking shelves with camping supplies, cartridges, and guns. In that part of God's country, hunting was more than the prominent hobby.

It supplied the townspeople with food as well as an opportunity to bond with nature and each other. The small town was set amid tall trees and vast, unmapped wilderness that was primed for discovery and talked about over beer and barbeque at the lone bar in town, the Balls Bluff Tavern.

The rustic establishment had seen just about everyone who had ever been born, lived, or died in the community.

The tavern marked the passage of time with laughter, fights, overreaching stories, and forgiveness of faults, but mostly it was the town's main meeting place.

They all toted guns into the bar but regardless of happenstance or alcoholic consumption, a gun seldom left its holster, or for those who'd rather carry a rifle, it leaned on a chair, never raised or cocked. The fights were usually among friends and regardless of how bad one friend beat another, the loser of the fight's gun remained secured, because through the blood, cussing, and mayhem, the thoughts of killing their neighbors harmed them far more than a fat lip, broken nose, or a temporarily bruised ego.

However, there was a family of brothers who didn't adhere to the norms of the establishment, or to the laws of common decency, for that matter.

The Kolb brothers were the worst kind of rednecks. When they entered the bar, the place nearly cleared out with the exception of the oldest and most ardent of drinkers.

They'd already lived a full life and a few young idiots didn't sway them into leaving before they had enough to make them forget their troubled and lonely existence. In most instances, community leaders told the state police to stand by in the parking lot when the Kolb brothers arrived at the tavern, because eventually there'd be trouble, and the fears of patrons lessened with a police presence. The Kolb brothers didn't fear the police, nor did they respect them or the laws they tried to enforce.

There were five Kolb brothers ranging in age from eighteen to twenty-five.

Everett, the youngest, was once a friend of Trent's. The middle three brothers, Wyatt, Kerry, and Morgan, were triplets but looked very different from each other and the eldest, Ethan, was the firstborn. Ethan, the eldest and worst of the brothers, felt that he deserved privilege and was untouchable because the people feared him the most. He caused many fights and beat many of the patrons of the bar to a pulp for merely questioning his choice in beers or his attire.

None of the Kolb brothers shaved, nor had they ever had a haircut, and baths were never a concern.

The Kolb family was the richest, and at one time, the most respected family in town because the patriarch, State Senator Randolph Kolb, excelled as a lifelong politician, businessman, and humanitarian.

Owning the majority of the land surrounding the town, Randolph had a hand in developing the town's charter years earlier. When he lost his wife during one harsh winter, he lost his desire to continue and retired to his multimillion-dollar mansion up on a hill overlooking the town, unseen and unheard of for many years. He neglected his sons, allowing them free reign over his empire, and they destroyed his good name through years of torturous activities and bad behavior.

Chapter 2
The Kolbs Terrorize

Many in town thought that the five brothers imprisoned their father in his house while others thought that he ran them out of his home at gunpoint. Ethan's brothers emulated their eldest sibling with various degrees of mischief until the townspeople feared them as much as they feared Ethan.

Ethan considered the town his own, felt entitled to anything he wanted, and became violent at the mere mention of payment for what he took in any of the various establishments around town.

Nancy, the fearless fulltime bartender and owner of the Balls Bluff Tavern, had had many altercations with Ethan and all of the Kolb brothers. Over the years, she knew his penchant for violence when drunk and unruly, which was most of the time.

Once, she delivered the bar bill to him, and he looked at her with an evil sneer, balled up the bill, and threw it in her face and cussing her out, "Fuck you! You fat bitch! I own this fucking shithole!"

Slurring his hateful words, he staggered out of the bar knocking bar stools over in his wake.

A strong-willed woman, Nancy fought him as she followed him out demanding payment many times but he never paid. The local police department consisted of a paid sheriff and a few volunteer deputies who had no jail because they worked out of an abandoned building.

They usually arrested those who skipped out on their bar bill and housed them in a locked bedroom, but even the police department feared the notorious brothers.

Many came to Nancy's defense in multiple prior altercations, but the regulars who were successful in getting him out of the bar paid a high price for their bravery the next day.

Ethan remembered those who manhandled him out of the bar through his drunken stupor and enacted a revenge designed to hurt for a long time.

A few years earlier, Ethan murdered Ben's childhood friend Jordy Penchant.

Jordy saw, firsthand, the extreme limits of Ethan's revenge. Elderly but strong, Jordy didn't take any crap from the Kolb brothers or anyone else, especially Ethan.

One night at midnight, bullets blasted through his bedroom window, hitting and killing his wife of thirty years.

Although he knew Ethan fired the shots, there was nothing he could do legally because of the ineptness of the police force, and for fear, the Kolb brothers would seek a deadly revenge, should they arrest their brother.

The leaders of the town wanted to enhance the police department, but soon the Kolb brothers' threats caused the leaders to back off that desire.

Ethan and his brothers threatened to burn down anything built to facilitate law and order. They allowed the abandoned building to stand because of the ease of escape.

Jordy, still grieving at the loss of his wife, walked right up to Ethan and his brothers' dilapidated old country home, and blasted two shots in the air to entice Ethan to come outside and face him. Ethan, seeing the old man reloading his shotgun, simply fired one bullet to the man's head, seriously wounding him.

Ethan dug a hole in the woods, unceremoniously pushed Jordy in it and shoveled dirt on the old man as he struggled to breathe. He laughed when he saw Jordy's last breath. The citizens of the town knew what Ethan had done but no one stepped up to bring him to justice because they feared the consequences.

Some attempted to call the State Police to investigate the murder, but it was hard to keep secrets in small towns, and soon, word got to Ethan about who called the authorities and the Kolbs viciously punished them.

Through burglary, beat-downs or murder, the Kolb brothers had many forms of revenge and used them all to insure that other residents didn't report the deeds of the Kolb brothers to state-level law enforcement personnel outside the town.

Ben's Sportsmen store fared much better against the Kolb brothers because Ethan always needed cartridges and the store was the only place within a hundred miles to get them.

The brothers tested Trent's father many times by loading up with ammunition without paying. Ben simply locked the door remotely to prevent Ethan's exit, drew his .44 Magnum pistol, and fired a shot just past his ear, blasting an easily repairable hole in the wall and causing Ethan to stop in his tracks.

"Ethan, you owe me $78.67 for your ammo. You're either leaving here after paying for what you're carrying, leaving here with nothing, or leaving in a box. Your choice!" exclaimed Ben. He cocked his revolver and pointed it at Ethan's head.

Ethan slowly pulled out his wallet without saying a word and gave Ben his credit card because he knew that Ben was perfectly prepared to end his life, and no one in town would care if they had one less Kolb brother to deal with.

"Ethan, you know I don't take credit cards. Cash or walk!" Ben demanded. He threw the card on the floor in front of him.

Ethan was afraid of no other man in town but he always shook hard when Ben had his gun pointed at him, because he knew that Ben wasn't as easy to push around as the other citizens were. Trent witnessed his father's bravery and backed him up with a shotgun behind the counter.

Ethan took out a hundred-dollar bill and asked, "Hey, Pritchard... Can I pick up my card on the floor?"

Ben smiled at Ethan's cowardly look and stated, "Sure. On second thought. That card didn't even have your name on it. You don't look like a Mary Anne."

With Ben busting him on the stolen credit card, Ethan slowly and carefully stooped down to collect the card, Ben blasted it with a .44 caliber round, obliterating the card and driving a multitude of splinters into Ethan's hand from the wooden floor.

Ethan recoiled against the wall, holding his hand up, and frightened, asked, "What the fuck, old man? I just wanted to pick up the card! You ruined it and look what you did to my hand!"

Ben smiled and said, "Dammit! I aimed for your hand! I'm going to have to adjust these sights! I gave you three choices earlier. What are you going to do, asshole?"

Ethan sheepishly handed him a hundred-dollar bill and collected his change. Ben remotely unlocked the door and he left hurriedly, cussing Ben and Trent under his breath and vowing revenge as he tried carrying his backpack with his splintered hand.

***

Young Trent knew firsthand about the Kolb brothers because he went to school with many of them, and once was even best friends with the youngest brother, Everett. The two went hunting and fishing together after school, and bonded quickly.

However, soon Everett emulated his older brothers and changed to be just as bad as they were, until all the good will he'd established for himself diminished to the level of all his brothers. Trent was proud of his father for standing up to Ethan, but sadly, Ethan had the last say.

Ethan broke into the store many times; each time, Ben waited for him with various pistols and rifles pointed at his head.

With every attempt, Ben nabbed him red-handed, and it incensed Ethan that he wasn't smart enough to outfox him, so he targeted Ben for assassination at a time of his choosing.

A rumor circulated around town that Trent's father hoarded cash somewhere in the store. The town didn't have a bank, so many of the merchants held onto cash until they made the trek to a bank in the neighboring town of Lost River.

Ethan and his brothers noticed that Trent's father made no trips to any bank for many months, so they thought that the shop held a huge stash of cash somewhere within it.

The Kolb brothers spent months planning an attempt to get it but first they had to subdue Ben, who seemed to know in advance of their invasions.

They crept up on the store at one o'clock in the morning hoping to catch Ben sleeping. They entered a side door leading to the living area and crept up some creaking stairs. They entered the master bedroom and saw Ben in bed asleep with Margie.

As they crept closer, Ethan heard the definitive sound of a shotgun cocking. Ethan turned around to see his brothers with their hands up. As they parted, Ethan saw Trent with a shotgun in both hands aimed at them all. "You have ten seconds to get out of here. I'm counting now. Everett, you know I'll pull the trigger."

Trembling with fear, Everett looked at Ethan and shook his head, agreeing that Trent would do as he said. The other three brothers took off and waited for their other two brothers in the parking lot of the outdoors store.

"Everett, get the fuck out of here!" Trent demanded.

Ben woke up and, as Ethan paid attention to the two shotguns pointed at him, he turned back to see Ben pointing his favorite pistol at him.

The anger in Ben's eyes caused them to run as fast as they could. Ben and Trent followed them out and blasted a few shots at their truck, destroying the taillights.

Ben turned to Trent. "I must be getting old. Ethan got the jump on me that time."

"Maybe, but not me. I heard them jimmy the side door and walk up the stairs."

"Thank you, son. I feel safe knowing you're here. Let's get back to bed. I don't think they'll be back tonight."

"Not tonight, but they will be back."

"I tell you, when I woke up, I nearly blasted them all. The town would have given me a medal."

***

Trent came across his boyhood friend many times after the robbery attempt.

Everett never went the way of his other brothers as a kid and appeared cordial and polite to the Pritchards, but when he was around Ethan, he was unrecognizable to Trent, which confused him greatly growing up.

***

Ben and Trent both thwarted many more attempts by the Kolb brothers to inflict a measure of revenge; Ben and Trent were always a few steps ahead of them.

Ben and Margie made plans to move to Florida and retire, grow oranges, and bask in the Florida sunshine.

However, they had to muddle through life in the small town for a few more years. Ben slowly groomed Trent to take over the shop.

Firstly, he taught him the business end of running his store, but Ben was quick to tell him that the citizens of the community were friends and he should treat them as such. Ben told him to relax the business aspect of the shop and extend credit to those he deemed worthy.

Trent, being highly intelligent, quickly picked up all facets of continuing the business. His father had complete confidence in his abilities to handle the Kolbs as well.

Trent met Amanda Hudson, Pastor Remington Hudson's daughter. She came into the store wanting to buy a tent.

The prettiest girl in town, the word around town was that she was enamored with Trent.

"Don't act like you don't know me, Trent Pritchard! You used to tease me in elementary school," she declared, as she eyed a folded-up tent on the top shelf.

"Amanda?" he asked, fumbling his words.

"Yes, that's right. I need a tent." She pointed to the tent she wanted to look at on the top shelf.

"Oh, sure! We have a few to choose from. How many people?"

Amanda replied, "Just me. I want to go out alone. It's so peaceful up on the mountain."

Trent, concerned, warned, "Going up there alone is dangerous. The bears are everywhere, not to mention the coyotes, and someone told me that they spotted a mountain lion as well."

"Oh, I'm taking my rifle just in case. I have to get up there to see the wildflowers bloom. I go to a certain spot every spring. Thanks for the concern, but I can take care of myself!"

"I have no doubt about that. Aren't you dating Ethan Kolb?" He climbed up, brought the tent down, and blew off some dust off the box.

"I used to date him but thank God I got out of it. He beat me all the time and wouldn't let me leave the house. He left the door unlocked once and I escaped, but he hasn't bothered me since I threatened to call the state police and have him arrested for kidnapping. He's one sick bastard."

"I know all about the Kolbs, but what made you want to date him?"

"Stupidity mostly, but he used to be very caring and nice when I was in grade school. He's older than I am and I guess that endeared him to me. Once his mother died and his father cut him off, he went berserk. Stealing, drinking, fighting, and screwing every woman in town. That's all he wanted to do and I got sick of it. Tell me something, Trent, do you have a girlfriend?" She asked sheepishly, faking that she was more interested in the tent than his answer.

Trent, seeing that she blushed asking the question, said, "Nope, not yet. I've been so busy at the store that I haven't had that much time to think about it. My parents are getting older so I have more responsibilities around here now."

"Do you know about The Knolls?" she asked, then spied the corner museum that his father set up. "What's that over there?"

Walking over to the small corner museum, she picked up an old book off the shelf.

"My father set it up. He had tons of stuff on the history of Red Dirt and rather than throw it out, he put it out for the customers. Yes, of course I know about The Knolls. My father always took me hunting up there. It's a beautiful place. Heck, most of the time we just went up there to talk about the town and the store. We seldom saw any deer."

She continued, "I'll be up there next Saturday and Sunday if you want to visit."

"Are you asking me out on a date, Amanda?" he asked, smiling broadly.

"Dammit! Trent, do I have to spell it out for you?"

"No, Amanda. I'm sorry. I've always wanted to go back up there. I haven't been there in years. It's a great time of year to explore, so…yes, I'll visit with you," he uttered, with a sheepish smile.

Amanda, having gotten her answer, purchased the tent. Trent completed the transaction, gave her change, and smiled as she left the shop flushed and happy.

Trent was extraordinarily happy knowing that Amanda appeared as if he interested her and couldn't wait to tell his parents about his weekend plans.

Trent said, "Mom, can you and Dad take over for me at the shop next weekend? I have a date!"

He nervously fiddled with his shirt.

"Sure, Trent. Who's the lucky girl?" she asked.

"Amanda Hudson. She wants to meet me at The Knolls next Saturday and possibly, Sunday."

"She's Remy's daughter. She's very pretty, son, but I thought that she was involved with one of those Kolb boys. You have to be careful if she still is," his mother stated.

She felt concerned that the Kolb brothers would enact some sort of terror on Trent if Amanda were still involved with one of them.

Trent explained, "Not any more, apparently. She told me earlier that she escaped the Kolbs and that lifestyle."

Margie responded, "I know her mother and father very well. Her dating that idiot nearly put her mother in her grave and her father threatened to disown her over it." She continued, "I'm so happy that she got away from them."

"So am I. I'm going to take a tent and some supplies. You can take them out of my earnings," he stated, as he wrote out his list.

His mother looked at him strangely and questioned, “Are you serious, sweetheart? All this is yours! You can take whatever you need. The business will be fine.”

Chapter 3
Trent's Nostalgic Trip

Trent thanked his mother.

A few days later he grabbed what he needed off the shelves. He was conscious about not taking the more expensive items, because he already had most of what he needed. Besides, the less he had, the less he'd have to carry up the mountain.

"Are you going to church with us tomorrow, dear?"

"Of course, Mom, but I don't know about next Sunday. Amanda may want me to stay with her up on the mountain."

"I envy you, dear, I love it up there!" Margie said, as she held Ben's hand.

Ben interjected and smiled, "I think that we can do the same thing, sweetheart, when Trent gets back."

"Yes, I'd love that!" Margie declared.

That Saturday turned out to be one of their busiest days of the year.

It was spring and many in town wanted to get away to the mountains, and Ben had the only store in town that accommodated their camping needs. The store served a steady stream of customers the entire day. They finally closed and sat back totaling the day's receipts.

"Wow, we did a lot of business today," Ben proudly stated.

Trent threw his work apron aside and stated, "I know, I'm tired. We're going to have to order a lot of supplies next week. We sold out of cartridges."

"I know, I'm tired as well. Maybe we should skip church tomorrow and sleep in," Margie suggested.

Ben stopped counting and answered, "No, we can't do that. Remy needs us there. People are not going to church anymore. Remy's been the pastor there well before the Kolb brothers started terrorizing the town. He's been my friend since we were nine. I can't let him down."

"It's not because the people don't want to go to church. It's those damn Kolb brothers. They know who goes to church and while the citizenry are there, they break into their homes and take whatever they can find. Soon, we'll not have a church. I pray that day does not come. You're right, we have to go!"

Margie stated, as she completed counting the money in front of her.

***

Sunday morning, the Pritchards left the store at eight o'clock and walked through the woods on a red dirt path to the church.

They could have driven, but Ben and Margie had been walking the path for the last thirty years, and never passed up the opportunity to spend time among nature and the tall trees with Trent strolling behind them.

Trent loved seeing them walk hand-in-hand through the woods as lovers.

Pastor Remington Hudson, whom Ben affectionately called Remy, met them at the old church's front door.

Margie was upset to see only ten people in the large main room. She harkened back to her youth as a little girl when her parents took her to church every Sunday to a full house. Remy's father had been a respected pastor, and the people loved it as he sermonized for hours, sang hymns, and generally loved being among the townspeople.

"God, I miss the days when I played on the floor while my parents sang hymns, and ate and played at the picnic afterward." She wiped a lone tear from her face.

"I remember, Margie. Look at Remy up there preaching as if it's a full house. I know this is killing him inside." Seated in a pew close to the front, Ben held Margie's hand.

"Since Jordy died, he's the only one who's still in my life. I miss my youth and all the fishing trips to old man Glover's pond with all of them. It's so sad how life turns out sometimes," he whispered, in a bittersweet tone.

Margie whispered back, "Please, Ben, we're in church and I'm trying to listen to Remy. We can discuss this after church."

"Oops, I'm sorry. You're right." Ben turned back to hear Remy's passionate request for the people present to ask their neighbors to return to the church. He even excoriated the Kolb brothers for inducing fear in the community.

They sat in the pew for two hours with Remy talking so much that it appeared that he lost his voice. His cracking tones resonated with the few that attended but his parishioners, as well as Ben and Margie, knew that he hurt inside.

The service ended, and the few people who attended, walked out the front door with Remy, thanking them for attending the service.

Ben and Margie were the last ones to leave, and Remy confided in his longtime friends.

"I don't know how long I can keep this up, Ben. I mean, the church doesn't bring in enough money to keep it open. Janie and I are barely making ends meet and the church has needed repairs for years but there's no money to fix it," the dejected and beaten down minister stated.

Margie looked at Ben, nudged him, and said, "Do it, sweetheart!"

"Do what?" Remy asked.

"Remy, I got a thousand dollars and I'd like to give it to the church." Ben put his arm around his friend.

Trent had a gift for Remy as well. "And I have another thousand for you, too!"

Remy, shaking his head, said, "I can't take it, I just can't take it. You, Margie, and Trent have been supporting this church, generously, for over two years. No, we'll turn it around when we get those Kolb brothers in here on Sundays. Once they find religion and come to the church, the people's fears will be relieved and they will return."

"Remy, we've been friends our entire life. Randy is sitting on millions of dollars up there on that hill. Why don't you ask him? You were the last one of us to see him," Ben suggested.

"I tried. I drove up there and knocked on his door and he never opened it. He's a very troubled man and certainly not himself since his wife died. I think dementia is setting in with him. No one ever sees him anymore; he even allows his sons to do what they do," Remy explained.

Trent sat back and listened to what the two old friends had to say, because Trent had an extraordinary interest in his father's past, given that he was friends with the richest and most mysterious man in the state.

"Hey, Ben, do you three want to join Janie and me at the tavern? I sincerely need a beer," Remy confessed.

"You don't drink anymore, Remy! Not that you ever drank much, but why now?"

"I know, but I'm feeling nostalgic; besides, God wouldn't judge me for having a beer or two with an old friend. I haven't been to the tavern in ten years. I wonder if Nancy's still there." Remy locked up the church.

"She's there; I went in last week. Sure! Why not! Margie doesn't drink but I'm sure she and Janie can talk about something and Trent and I haven't had a beer together. He's eighteen now so I think it's about time. " He looked at Trent. "What do you say, Trent? You want to have a beer with your old man?"

"I went there last week too, but I'd like that."

Trent smiled and thanked him for including him. They walked two blocks to the Balls Bluff Tavern, entered, and saw Nancy behind the bar.

"Pastor Hudson, it's been ages since you've been in here. Hi, Janie, I haven't seen you in many years as well. What can I get for you?" She placed napkins on the table at all five seats.

They all sat down. Ben said, "Let me have a Coors Light and a Diet Coke for my wife here."

"We'll have the same, Nancy," said Remy.

"Trent, do you want your usual?" Nancy asked as she wrote down the orders on her pad.

"That would be great, Nancy."

Ben noticed an elderly man in the corner nursing his beer who'd stared at him ever since he sat down.

“Who is that old man in the corner, Remy?” Ben asked.

“I don’t believe it! You don’t recognize him?”

“No, should I?” asked Ben.

Remy laughed and said, “That’s old man Glover!”

“Glover? The man who owned the fishing pond way back when? He’s got to be pushing a hundred!”

“He’s ninety-four, to be exact. He’s got a lot of mental issues since…you know… that day,” Remy reminded.

Janie and Trent obviously didn’t know what they were talking about and Janie asked, “What day? What happened?”

Remy held up his hand to Ben and said, “I’ll tell her.”

“Sweetheart, a long time ago, us kids used to go fishing every week. Ben and Margie here, Jordy, Patch, Randy, and me. After school, we all met at a certain spot on the banks of old man Glover’s pond. He constantly yelled at us to leave his property, sometimes chasing us all the way home. One day, we all met at the same spot but old man Glover hid in the bushes and as soon as we threw our lines in the water, he pounced on us. Jordy, Patch, Randy, and I got away but he caught Ben and threw him in the pond. Well, he didn’t know that Ben couldn’t swim at the time and he sank like a stone. “

Janie stated, “That’s horrible!”

Remy continued, "Glover jumped in to try to save him but he couldn't find him and thought that he'd drowned. He left to get help but Patch watched from the bushes, jumped in and pulled Ben out, saving his life. He located Ben when his head bobbed above the surface. That old man still thinks that Ben drowned, even though I've tried to convince him for years that you were still alive. The man is so distraught because he thought he killed a small boy, he went into a depression that had serious mental effects on him. To this day, he still thinks Ben drowned that day."

Trent said, "Dad, you told me that story earlier but you failed to mention that old man Glover threw you in."

Ben said, "I honestly don't remember him throwing me in. I just didn't think it was that important how it happened. I'm here now because of Patch."

As Remy finished his story, the old man finished his beer, slowly got up from his seat in the dark corner of the bar, and walked toward Ben's table.

"Hello, Mr. Glover," stated Ben.

Glover stopped as he passed by their table.

"Hello, Pastor." He pointed at Ben. "I will not talk to you!"

Ben asked, "Why not?"

The bearded Glover said, "Because you're not real. You're a ghost, Ben Pritchard. I threw you in the pond and you drowned. I saw you under the water! Your eyes were open and you weren't breathing because I couldn't get your foot free of those underwater branches. You were dead when I left. I went to your funeral. I saw them lower you in the ground! You're not real!" he screamed.

"But he is real, Mr. Glover! He's sitting right there in the chair and this is his son, Trent," Remy stated.

Mr. Glover looked at Trent and said, "You can't exist either because your father died forty years ago. The only way you could be here is if someone went back in time and changed things. Since that can't happen, you must be a ghost as well!"

Remy looked at Ben in disbelief and remarked, "I've told you, Mr. Glover, a friend of ours jumped in and pulled him out. You've spent forty years spouting that nonsense. Patch saved Ben that day and he's sitting right there."

"He's got you hypnotized, Pastor. I know what I saw and I remember how I felt. I see his face under water every day! He's dead!" He looked at Trent and continued, "I'm sorry, son, but you were never born and I should be in prison for what I did."

Glover left the table, convinced that Ben and Trent didn't exist, which was the cause for an hour of conversation on the subject.

Trent remarked, "That guy's insane, Dad."

Remy interjected, "You may be right, Trent, but consider that he thought he killed a child. He's been punishing himself ever since. He's old and troubled and his mind is leaving him. I've tried to talk to him but I feel that the death of his wife is the actual cause of his dementia. She died that same year. We all just allow him to think the way he thinks."

Ben said, "I just know that Patch pulled me out and I woke up with him pushing on my chest. That is the last day I fished that pond. I don't even remember Glover throwing me in the pond. Does he still own it?"

"Yes, he's still at the same old house, but the water level in the pond is real low now. I drove out his way to check on him and saw him at the same spot where we fished, muttering to himself. He even placed a special marker there on a tree about the incident," Remy explained.

"A marker?" Trent asked.

"It's nothing special. Just an inscription on a nearby tree. People say that it keeps him alive because he visits there daily and prays for his salvation. He thinks God is allowing him to stay alive by reliving that day to pay penance for what he thinks he did," Remy explained.

"Dad, can we go there? I'd like to see the tree and the spot," Trent confessed.

"Wednesday, son. I'd like to see it myself. Wow, I haven't been there since the incident. I hope I can still find it." Ben sipped his beer. "Well, Remy, I've had fun reminiscing, but I think it's time to go. I have to get back to the store to figure out what we have to order. We sold out of a lot of things yesterday."

Ben asked Nancy for the tab. "I got this, Remy. You got the tab last time."

"Yes, I did, ten years ago. You have a great memory, Ben."

"Well, you remembered it, too," he reminded.

"That's because I paid for it," he responded, with a huge smile on his face.

They went their separate ways. The Pritchard's took their time walking on the red dirt path back to their home.

Trent looked forward to two events. He constantly thought about his date with Amanda the following weekend, and he and Ben made plans to go to that fishing spot on Wednesday. Ben chose Wednesday because Remy told him that Mr. Glover wouldn't be there, because he visited his daughter in the next county on Wednesdays.

Ben feared that if Glover saw him and Trent at that spot, he might become disoriented, and bring out his shotgun.

***

They ordered all their supplies for the shop, which arrived Wednesday morning.

They all spent the day restocking the shelves but Trent thought about his and Ben's excursion to Glover's pond after the store closed.

A very slow day, they decided to close an hour early. After they totaled the receipts for the day, the two took off for the pond.

They arrived a half-hour later at a point where their car could go no farther. They parked and hiked the rest of the way on a seldom used path, similar to the one that they walked on going to church.

"This used to be a dirt path that we kids made a long time ago. Most of it has grown over. I'm surprised anything grew on that red clay underneath it but it did," Ben explained.

"I wish I'd have brought my machete; this is pretty thick through here," Trent observed.

"Hey, we were only four feet tall. The underbrush folded over like a tunnel back then, but the path is just dirt. Well, back then the roads were dirt as well. That's why we called the town Red Dirt. Nothing paved existed anywhere around this town."

"Are we close?"

"Yes, we're close. There it is! Wow, the water level is low but this is the spot where we fished. You see a marker anywhere?" Ben asked.

"Here it is! Over here on the tree!"

Walking over to the large tree, Trent read the worn engraving. With the outer bark stripped away, they saw a smooth writing surface. Glover had burnt the inscription into the tree. It read:

Here is where I killed a boy. I think about what I did every day. I will not forgive myself because I deserve no forgiveness. The penitence I pay is to remember that day, every day, for the rest of my life. My life ended this day. Benjamin Pritchard 1960-1971.

"Wow, that day really affected Glover, didn't it?" Trent placed his hands on the bare tree trunk.

"That poor man. He's been beating himself up over this for a long time. I'm really sorry that I can't put his mind at ease. Oh well, are you ready to get back to the shop?" he asked.

Just as Trent was ready to answer, Glover plodded his way through the brush to see Ben and Trent by his tree.

"What are you ghosts doing by my tree?" he asked angrily, and raised his shotgun in their direction.

"If you think we're ghosts, that shotgun's not going to do you any good. We've come back to release you from your pain," Ben said.

Trent glanced at his father with a strange look on his face.

"Go with me on this, Trent," he whispered.

"You're here to release me? Did God send you here, son?" Glover lowered his gun.

Ben stated, "Yes, we're here to let you know that you don't have to feel pain anymore. You've paid your penance. You can live the rest of your life free of guilt."

He noticed tears and a sigh of great relief from Glover.

"I should have been in jail for what I did. I turned myself in but they didn't charge me with your murder. I deserved it. I prayed to God that he'd send me to prison to pay for my sin. Then they said that you didn't die, but I knew better," the sullen man explained.

Ben noticed small trickles of tears running down the lined face of the old man and also a big smile as he sat on a stump and put his head in his hands and said, "I'm so sorry I threw you in the lake, son. You were not allowed to grow up in our living world because of me."

Ben walked over to the hurting man and simply said, "I forgive you."

Glover replied, "Thank you, Ben. I've always prayed that you'd say that. I have to leave now because my wife is waiting for me."

He stood up and waved goodbye to Ben and Trent.

They watched Glover walk away through the woods. They left as well, but not before Ben reflected on what Glover said.

"Amazing that a man like Glover had such a deep-seated passion for paying for something that didn't happen." He slashed a bush that blocked his path.

Trent, also removing brush from his path, said, "I don't know, Dad. For a while, there he had me convinced that you actually did die in the pond. He still believes it even though you stood right in front of him."

"He thinks I'm a spirit, son. The poor man has lost his mind. I guess a traumatic moment in a person's life will do that to a man's reason. Months later, I went with my mother to the grocery store and his wife stopped and talked to my mother. I remember talking to her then and a few other times before she died and she told me that he woke up in the middle of the night thinking about that day all the time. It's got to be a tremendous burden to live with the fact that he may have killed a child."

They arrived at the car and Trent asked, "What did he mean when he said that he had to get back to his wife. I thought the pastor said that she died."

"She did. I don't know what's going on in that old man's mind. We have to get home. Your mom's probably got dinner ready."

They drove back to the shop. Margie was cleaning up in the kitchen with dinner ready and waiting for her men to arrive back home.

The day left a great impression on Trent as he saw his father reason with a man who was obviously delusional and made the broken old man feel as if God released all the pain locked in his heart.

There was nothing he could say to Glover to make him believe that he didn't die so long ago, so Ben used Glover's obvious mental illness and allowed him to view him as a spirit who God sent back to relieve his pain. It proved to be the only way to release him from his troubled past.

***

The next two days went by fast.

Friday night, after they closed the store, his mother and father sat on the back deck to experience a glorious cloud-free night sky full of stars with a gentle warm wind that caressed his mother's blonde hair.

Trent came in and sat with them.

His mother held Ben's hand and said, "Did you know that The Knolls is where your father and I met?"

"No, I didn't." Trent agreed because she'd told him that multiple times but he didn't want to hurt her feelings. He retrieved a pitcher of lemonade from the refrigerator and set it on a nearby table for the three of them.

Ben explained further. "I led the search party looking for your mother who got lost up there. We searched for two days over the whole mountain but I found her so I got to keep her."

Margie added, "When I heard Ben calling out for me, I thought that I died and heard things. I'd broken my leg running away from a bear. It batted me around for a bit but I played dead and it went away. I couldn't walk and yelled so loud that I lost my voice. But you heard me didn't you, baby?" She gently and sweetly kissed Ben on his cheek.

"Yep, it's so quiet up there. It's sort of difficult to not hear a woman crying. I got her unstuck, made a quick splint, and carried her down the mountain. After all that work, there was no way that I was going to let her go," Ben explained, with a smile toward his wife.

Margie asked, "I love that story. Trent, when are you leaving for The Knolls?"

"I haven't decided whether or not I can go. Are you guys going to be all right at the store? Spring is the busiest time of the year."

"We'll be fine, it's only one day. I guess you won't be here for church Sunday morning. I know it's going to be a beautiful weekend weather-wise, so we'll be busy, but your father and I can handle it fine. You go enjoy yourself," she remarked.

"I don't know, Mom. I think she wants me to stay overnight with her. Besides, I don't want to leave her there alone. It may be a nice place but it's still dangerous," he explained.

Ben nodded his head in agreement.

"Okay, I understand. I just assumed that since Amanda is the pastor's daughter that she wanted to attend," she suggested, as she sipped her lemonade.

Trent was a great son and an even better worker. He knew how to handle the Kolb brothers on his own, since he'd grown up to be a strong man who towered over many of them.

He learned from his father how to handle them when they came in the store drunk and belligerent. He had no fear of them when they tried to steal and threaten to get their way.

He was concerned because his parents were getting older and the weekend was a favorite time for the Kolb brothers to terrorize people.

It also concerned him that Ethan and his brothers, were able to break into their home unobserved the last time they tried.

The Kolbs visited the store every weekend for ammunition, because of their weekend gunplay at their house in the woods.

They all lived in the same house about two miles from their father's home. Their dilapidated home, situated on their father's land and built in the early 1900s, was supposed to be torn down years earlier because of the trash and hazard of it possibly falling down on its own. Each brother had his own room in the two-story home. Littered in the front yard, were various junk cars, car parts, old rusted appliances, and thousands of empty beer cans strewn throughout the property. It was where they hung out and drank themselves dumb.

In the center of it all was a fire pit with various old lawn chairs surrounding it.

This was where they'd have their weekly beer parties. They invited all their girlfriends as well as other young, underage girls and blasted country music until the wee hours of the morning, causing mischief with every passing hour.

They made a game out of any unfortunate animal, domestic or wild, that wandered too close to the party. They mercilessly shot the animals multiple times just so the brothers could see them suffer.

They placed bets among them who could kill the animal with the least amount of shots fired. In their drunken stupor, they took chances by shooting their guns toward each other or their girlfriends to display their marksmanship when there were no small animals around.

Many a time, the Kolb brothers injured the girls due to their juvenile displays, but the brothers didn't care because the town had a reasonable supply of young, impressionable, bored girls looking for excitement, and the Kolb house had a never-ending supply of excitement.

When the Kolb brothers couldn't amuse themselves at their house, they liquored up and took their gun show to town, terrorizing its inhabitants. They shot out streetlights and the people scurried to take cover from the broken glass streaming down upon them.

The local storeowners implored their customers to stay inside until the brothers moved on because the citizens had very little stomach to stop them.

The Pritchards ate a large dinner and retired for the night. Trent had a long day ahead of him, but as he lay in his bed, he thought about the old man and all that he'd said to them on the banks of the pond.

He was amazed at how vivid the memories were in Glover's mind and how convinced he seemed that his father had indeed died.

He fell asleep quickly as he dreamt about the coming weekend and his date with Amanda.

***

Waking up the next morning refreshed and ready to start his day, Trent's mind was elsewhere. Constantly ringing up the wrong prices, and seemingly forgetting where certain items were in the store, Margie knew what was on his mind and offered him the rest of the day off but he'd have none of that.

He got through that day and the next, but that night he couldn't sleep in anticipation of the next morning and his date with Amanda. He hoped that the weather cooperated because The Knolls supplied breathtaking vistas that were a perfect combination coupled with his breathtaking date.

Waking up groggy, he needed coffee and a quick breakfast before readying himself for his day.

With very little sleep, Trent nervously loaded up everything he needed in his truck, including a pistol and his shotgun. He felt wary of leaving his parents to tend to the store alone because he knew that the Kolb brothers would visit to buy more cartridges, or attempt to steal them.

Still, he liked Amanda, and he also needed time away from the store, so he set out for The Knolls at six o'clock Saturday morning. While driving to the mountain, he wondered what the weekend would bring.

Looking down, he saw he was driving ninety miles an hour. "Easy, Trent," he said to himself, as he slowed down to sixty-five and turned on the radio to help him cope with the seemingly slow pace. Driving into the parking area, he saw her distinctive bright red Jeep.

He parked next to it, went to the back of his truck, and gathered his huge backpack and his rifle.

It was a daunting trek up the mountain, but he'd been up there so many times that the climb proved easy for him; besides, he had a beautiful woman waiting for him at the end of the well-worn path, which made for a seemingly short trip.

In walking up the red dirt trail, he saw what Amanda described about the wildflowers. They exploded everywhere with all the colors of the rainbow, and scented the clean air with nature's bouquet.

He stopped for a breather at a favorite spot where his father and mother met and saw the inscription on a tree commemorating their meeting. Given the town's proximity, cellphone service was sparse, but up in the mountains, it worked well enough to make a static-filled call or two.

He called his father. "Hello, Dad, I'm at your spot up here. How are things at the store?"

"Great. I bet the view is beautiful. I'm going to have to take your mother up there before the spring is over. Have you seen any bears yet?"

Trent heard him interacting with a customer.

"No, no bears but I did see a few whitetails," he proudly noted.

"No shit; did you get a shot off?" Ben asked.

"This is not a hunting trip, Dad. Besides, I'm just not in the hunting mood. Have the Kolb brothers been in yet?" Trent removed his backpack and placed it on a large bolder.

"Yes, but not Ethan. Morgan bought a lantern, some oil, and a few other things. I can take care of myself, son. Don't worry about us. You enjoy your weekend, okay." Ben reassured Trent but said that he had to go because he had customers to tend to.

"Okay, I love you. Tell Mom that I made it. Goodbye, Dad, I want to get to the top of the mountain early."

"Okay, be careful and remember there are bears up there with cubs," he reminded him as he hung up.

Trent placed his phone in his backpack.

The sun was up and blazing in the clear sky. Walking up the trail, he noticed many small animals, and some followed him on his journey, seemingly unafraid of him. He knew he shouldn't do it but he sprinkled some bread crumbs along the way.

The animals supplied him with company and he enjoyed them scampering about collecting the bread morsels. He fashioned a walking stick out of an old broken branch, and up the hill he walked until he saw the treeless green meadow atop the mountain, awash with blooming flowers for as far as the eye could see, and the smell of spring in the air was impossible to ignore.

In the distance, he saw Amanda's small tent halfway obscured by the tall grass.

"Amanda," he called out as she stood up. Her long blonde hair blew across her face in the gentle wind.

She wore a white flowing dress with hiking boots and a few wildflowers in her oversized white spring hat, accenting her beauty.

Seeing Trent approach, she noticed that he was dressed in a camouflage-type shirt and shorts, mountain boots, and an old leather hat that appeared to have seen many adventures.

She ran to him through the tall grass with the sun shining behind her and holding her hat as she ran with the sun blasting through her white dress, displaying her perfectly sculpted silhouette.

"Hi, Trent, I hoped you'd show up. I've been here for hours waiting for you." She wrapped her arms around him in greeting.

"Hours? Seeing you in this setting sure does enhance the beauty of this place. That dress against the green grass is striking," he nervously said.

"Thank you. I love this dress. By the way, did you get a good view of my body when the sun shone through it? I know you were watching," she stated with a wry smile.

"I just thought I was incredibly lucky. Yes I did, and I thank you for the experience," he confessed.

"That's another reason why I like this dress. Come on, let's set up your tent next to mine. Then we can go hiking down by the river. What a glorious day" she said, smiling.

They set up his tent fast as he wondered whether or not he'd actually use it, because hers was a much larger model, made for two where his was simply a one-man pup tent. That thought depended on how the rest of the day progressed.

He walked beside her and his hand glanced off hers a few times until she grabbed his and held on.

She noticed how nervous he seemed so she took the lead, and afterward he always grabbed her hand first.

They reached the small clearing she made. She had a radio that delivered soft music to the setting.

Acres and acres of knee-high white foamflowers, honeysuckle, and purple wild geraniums surrounded them.

He sat down next to her as she gave him a bottle of red wine and a corkscrew and gathered up two wine glasses. He quickly popped the cork and poured wine into the crystal glasses, but he couldn't take his eyes off her and spilled it as her glass overflowed.

"It's full!" she said, and smiled at Trent's obvious clumsiness.

Chapter 4
Reality Finds Trent

He stopped pouring and swabbed the drops of wine on her dress. She took a few sips from her glass to decrease the amount of wine in the glass.

Putting the bottle down, the spillage no longer concerned him, as she stared deeply into his soul with eyes that seared right through to it.

He knew then and there that he loved her.

No, this is too quick, he thought, but he couldn't resist any longer and he reached over and kissed her gently on the lips. Pulling away, he thought that he might have ruined the moment for her by his untoward advance. Sipping her wine, she smiled shyly, and returned the kiss, although hers lasted much longer, filled with passion and the sweet taste of the grapes' nectar.

They decided to stay at the campsite for a few hours talking about anything and everything.

Always having something to say, she peppered stray kisses into their talk which made the conversation much more interesting.

Amanda looked out over the expansive property sipping her wine and uttered, "This is amazing. I could stay up here forever."

Trent spied movement at the tree-line and pointed. "It's pretty up here. Look! Down in the valley. A mother bear and her two cubs!"

"I don't see anything," she said, placing her wine glass on the small table next to her chair.

"Here, look through these. They're right over there."

He handed her a pair of binoculars and pointed to the tree line.

"Beautiful. I don't want to go near them and I hope they stay down there, but they're beautiful to look at from a distance," she said, as she took another look.

After hours of talking about each other's lives, Trent stood and helped her up as she continued to watch the bears through the binoculars.

"You ready to go hiking?"

"Oh, yes, I'm ready. I need to put some water in my backpack. Do you think I'll need to take my gun?" she asked, as she pulled it from her tent.

"Well, I've got mine. You probably don't need it but you should take it anyway, just in case someone strolls by our camp. They'll take it in a heartbeat."

Placing his old hiking hat on his head, he grabbed his makeshift walking stick.

"What is that on your head?"

He removed the floppy hat. "My dog found it not too far from here during a hunting trip last year. It's cool, isn't it?"

"It looks really old. It's an odd color."

She playfully grabbed it from his hand and modeled it herself.

"It's stained leather and fits tight, but it stays put during a strong wind and it keeps the sun out of my eyes," he explained. He took it from her and placed it back on his head.

"It almost looks like blood on it. I've got my own hiking hat." She modeled her large white floppy hat.

"Well, at least mine blends into the scenery," he said, laughing.

"I've got to change into my shorts though."

She boldly removed her dress in front of him, not worrying about what he thought or saw.

"Trent, you're staring!" she said, with a broad smile on her face.

He turned away, embarrassed and said, "It's kind of tough not looking."

"Good, I don't want you to turn away. Does my body look the same as it did when the sun shined through my dress?" she asked.

She changed into an oversized shirt and long shorts.

"Exactly," he said, as he stared, transfixed on her extraordinary body.

"Okay, I'm ready."

Helping her with her backpack, he handed her favorite hat to her.

Amanda had her camera with her; she studied to be a nature photographer for two years at the local college a town away. She wanted to capture everything, and taking pictures was her way of preserving the moments of her life.

Trent wanted to see if she thought that the ones they experienced were memorable ones, by the amount of pictures she took of him. They walked for an hour into the forest and found a small, trickling shallow creek. The water, chilled and clear due to nature's rejuvenating cleansing, as the springtime temperatures released the mountain's melting snow, ended in the flowing creek. Amanda took her boots off, waded in, knelt down on flat rocks, and cupped some water in her hand, bringing it up to her mouth to drink.

"It tastes so clean, Trent. Come out here and try it."

Placing his large backpack and rifle on the bank, he waded out with his boots on, sat on an adjacent rock, and did as Amanda requested. It was an extraordinarily and unusually warm spring afternoon of seventy-eight degrees. However, Trent took a sip and noted that the water still possessed winter's chill.

Playfully pushing him into the two-foot-deep creek, Amanda laughed heartily to see Trent catch his breath in the chilly water. He stood up and feigned anger as his old hat floated past him. He gathered his hat. However, the hat filled with water, and gave him an additional frigid douse as he placed it on his head, which made them explode with laughter.

Seeing Trent soaked to the skin, Amanda waded over to him and kissed him amid the slow-running stream, without worrying or caring about getting wet herself. Trent, seeing the perfect opportunity, picked her up and kissed her, seemingly wanting to take her ashore, but instead he threw her in the deepest part of the creek. She stood up, the two stared at each other, and they laughed at the romantically awkward moment. The cool water chilled them to the bone; they walked out of the creek, removed their clothes, and placed them on the sun-warmed rocks to dry them out.

They fell in love with each other during their frolicking in the creek, because they walked and talked in their underwear and neither thought of making love by the creek.

Amanda was topless and Trent stripped down to his shorts. Though they both fought the urge, they knew it would happen before the day was over, and doing it on the rocky banks of the creek proved impossible. They looked at it as a precursor for a more comfortable setting. Their clothes dried quickly, and they continued their hike a few hours later.

They encountered many animals on their way toward the unknown, but Trent didn't feel the need to raise his rifle once. They spent the better part of the day on the glorious trek but needed to return to their camp before dusk, because the dangers of the mountain come out at night and they wanted to be at the camp before all of it started.

Walking on a worn path back to camp, he contemplated that they'd left for the hike as strangers, wondering about each other, only to return as lovers, knowing everything, though they hadn't consummated their love for each other and the anticipation of it enhanced their desire to get back. As they walked, they spied a bear sitting in their path. It reared up when it saw them walking toward it. The bear ran toward them as Trent raised his rifle and fired one shot.

***

Sadly, the shot brought him out of his deep sleep, but being on the mountain with Amanda wasn't a dream he conjured up. He reminisced about his first date with his now wife, Amanda, to counter his seriously terrifying situation.

Everything he experienced in his mind up to that point was a memory. His father, Glovers pond, church, the store; he remembered it all. He remembered that time to relax his mind because, in reality, he was not in the glorious setting in the mountains with Amanda.

His thoughts always reverted to that time on the mountain with her when he was in a tense and troublesome situation.

No, his real situation was much different. Trent dreamed, and his dreams were so vivid that, once remembered, he relived those times as if they actually happened all over again.

He remembered his first date fondly with his future wife, and that was when he woke up. However, it stung him when he woke up to realize that he still lay in the same hellish dark box, buried four feet underground.

The remembrances of his first date with Amanda calmed him in his dark, tight, prison with his tormentors nearby, shooting their guns and disrupting his beautiful memories.

Trent had been kidnapped, drugged, shot, and buried. Everything up to that point was him reliving his past to calm him in his hellish predicament. His unseen kidnappers had placed him there days prior. Two four-inch diameter PVC pipes supplied him with air and were his only lifelines with the aboveground world.

Suspecting that the Kolb brothers were responsible for his predicament, he had no way of knowing for sure, since he didn't recognize any of the muffled voices, he heard prior to them burying him alive.

Having a small flashlight with him, he managed to turn it on to see what his environment looked like in his very confined space.

Many times, he hoped that his imaginative mind conjured his reality but it always proved exactly like the first time he woke up in the box.

The pain caused by his injuries ceased hurting after a while because he got used to the pain and didn't hurt as much anymore, but his confinement caused him to stiffen up.

The hastily built box creaked because of the massive pressure of the impacted soil on top of it, and he felt it grow weaker when he pushed on the sides or the top.

He didn't panic too much because his kidnappers obviously wanted him alive; otherwise, why supply him with air outlets? he thought.

And every once in a while, a bottle of water and some smashed bread made its way down one of the PVC pipe near his head.

The box didn't allow a lot of room to move around in, and without his flashlight on, it was completely black save a small bit of light that shone through the PVC pipes at the front and rear of the box.

The kidnappers outfitted one of the PCV pipes with a small battery-operated fan to suck out carbon dioxide, which sucked in breathing air from the other pipe. He'd suffered a terrible year prior to his kidnapping and there were times that, in his desperation, he wanted to end it all, remove the PVC pipes, turn off his flashlight, and die a slow death in his makeshift coffin. His limits reached their pinnacle as he remembered his recent past.

The death of a child, a wife, and two loving parents in a short period of time tested those limits. Still, he persevered through the barbs and took their jagged edges with grace and humility.

A husband at twenty and a father at twenty-eight, he found out that happiness occurred when souls collide to form a euphoria designed to see him through a lifetime with a perpetual smile on his face and an eternal hope that his unborn child and his wife wouldn't have to trek the same path of thorns that he had.

Sadly, life isn't fair and even the most benevolent man can be thrust into the world of murder, revenge, and a belief that those who commit such vile acts should be subject to the same torturous path.

They imprisoned him for money and revenge, given the kidnappers' muffled demand that he tell them where his father hid the money within the Sportsmen store. The Kolb brothers were a constant terror to Trent and the store since a certain occurrence a year earlier.

Closing his eyes, he remembered the silence of the brothers digging his grave when he woke up after someone knocked him out. Thinking back to before they buried him, he remembered lying on his side with his hands bound and a bag over his head. Conscious and still, he hoped to pick up any kind of information as to what they were going to do to him. He could barely see through the burlap bag; however, he lay too far away to discern, definitively, who his kidnappers were.

They were silent when they picked him up and placed him in the box but Trent still feigned that he was unconscious. He sensed that they didn't place the top onto the box right away because he felt the slight gust of wind through the porous sack on his head, and he heard three different voices and beer cans opening a short distance away. Two of the men argued but Trent couldn't understand why they argued.

Suddenly, a gunshot rang out, followed by a stabbing pain in his back. He attempted to make no sounds, nor did he acknowledge the pain to warrant another bullet to his back. He laid in serious agony and pulled out every bit of strength he had to refrain from flinching. The pain only lasted a few seconds, so Trent figured that the bullet might have just grazed him.

He moved both his legs and arms, covertly, to check on their mobility.

Chapter 5
Trent's Plan

There were other shots fired, but luckily for Trent not in his direction, because he didn't feel the bullets' impact anywhere near him. He heard his kidnappers throwing their beer cans at him as they approached, with two of the cans landing in the box where he'd lain for an undetermined amount of time.

Struggling to free himself at that juncture proved futile because they had bound him tightly, there were more of them than of him, and they had shot him.

He decided to allow them to do what they wanted and hoped that they'd think he was dead and leave him where he was.

Speculating that they'd inflict additional injury if he resisted, he remained calm. He needed all his limbs working once they decided to bury him if that was indeed part of their plan.

So, he remained as still as he could. He counted on their lack of intelligence and their inability to see any potential error in their plan to capitalize on.

Trent was thankful that they didn't clear his pockets of his small flashlight and pocketknife.

He needed all his tools to try to escape once the kidnappers left the area. The Kolbs were never ones to use their heads and he counted on their stupidity to overlook things. Saying nothing further, they placed the top on the box, and Trent heard the shovelfuls of dirt plopping upon the lid.

Trying to count them, to somehow determine how deep they buried him, proved futile when they thrust enough shovels full of dirt into the hole where it no longer made sounds, so he discounted the idea. He overheard someone, who sounded like Morgan, stating that he wanted to find his father's safe, hidden in his house attached to the Sportsmen store, and they needed him out of the way until they searched for it. They knew that Trent now had no family and no employees and thought that they could easily portray themselves as workers to make the search less suspicious to prying eyes.

Trent's keys were missing, so they had free reign to search his house at their leisure, and to also gut the store of its inventory.

Thinking back to just a day earlier, to his tortuous time prior to being buried, didn't help the situation, but his thoughts veered to happier times, which lessened the panic setting in and calmed him, supplying him with the ability to think of a way out of his predicament. Releasing his hands, he removed the burlap sack from his head.

The top of the box lay a mere four inches from his nose and less than that to his chest. His arms had more room but the obvious claustrophobic nature of his confinement caused a mild panic in his troubled mind.

The first day, he used his time screaming for help and struggling to move around in his tight, tiny prison but couldn't muster the strength necessary to make even a feeble attempt at freeing himself.

Panic set in hours later when it became obvious that he couldn't escape. His heart's rapid beat didn't help as he realized that no one was looking for him or coming for him. Forcing himself to calm his nerves despite the dire nature of his situation, he settled down, placed his hands on his stomach, closed his eyes, and remembered where he left off on his mountaintop date with Amanda because it soothed him.

***

That was where his story began, and the thoughts of the last few years of heartbreak possibly supplied him with enough rage and courage necessary to help him escape.

Stopping his futile attempts, he took a few deep breaths to calm his drum-rolling heartbeat, and remembered.

Settling down within the box, he closed his eyes, and continued his story of his past. He finished remembering his first date with Amanda from the blast at the bear that barreled toward them. He remembered that he had missed the bear with his shot, but it stopped dead in its tracks and ran through the woods with her two baby bears right behind her.

Amanda was both fearful and proud of Trent because he didn't kill it, though he easily could have and eradicated the threat.

Walking for hours, the trees opened to a small river with its clean water briskly moving past them. They were ready to explore the river when he and Amanda came under fire from the adjacent bank.

They had just made it to the river when the shots rang out and narrowly missed them. The bullets ricocheted off the many rocks around them and slightly grazed Trent's arm.

"Who's out there?" he yelled.

There was no reply other than another gunshot that again ricocheted off a rock and into the stream. Trent saw where the shot came from, raised his rifle, and aimed.

Amanda placed her hand on the barrel of Trent's gun and lowered it. "Suppose they're just hunters, Trent."

"Amanda, they shot at us twice. We don't look like deer. Plus, I called out to them and they didn't reply. We're also wearing hunter's vests. They shot at us, plain and simple. Just stay down behind these rocks and I'll go find out what's going on."

He took his gun and walked up the hill while Amanda stayed behind the rocks and feared for them both.

After a short while, Amanda heard a few more shots and saw Trent stumbling toward her, bleeding from his abdomen.

"Oh dear God, you've been shot!" Amanda frantically helped him behind the rocks.

"It's not as bad as you think. The bullet is a low caliber and my belt slowed it down a lot. I don't think it went in me that much. I'll be all right. I never found the guys who shot at us but I heard them running off into the woods. I think we're safe now. Well, we'd better get back to the truck. I have to get to a doctor just in case I'm wrong in my assessment of my wound."

"Okay, let's go now. I have a confession. Ethan knew that we were coming here," she informed, as she helped him up.

"How did he find out that?"

"He confronted me at the general store this morning and I told him, but I didn't think that he'd do this." She opened his shirt to see his wound and assess how bad it looked.

"Yep, that's who shot me. I'd bet anything. Well, I'm sure he's gone now since I returned fire. Let's go to the camp and gather everything up."

"To hell with that stuff, we have to get you to a hospital!" demanded Amanda.

She tried to stop the bleeding by ripping a piece of Trent's shirt and holding pressure on the wound.

Trent reiterated that the wound was superficial and countered, "No, we have to go back and get your stuff. I'll be fine. Look, here's the bullet. It just fell out."

He presented her with the bloody bullet.

They made great time in getting back to their camp and Trent seriously thought of not leaving at all, considering the bleeding had stopped and the bullet had extracted itself. However, when he expressed that sentiment, Amanda took charge and nixed the idea immediately.

Trent helped her carry her things and they quickly made their way back down the mountain.

Walking toward their vehicles, they found Trent's truck's windshield shot out and he knew a jealous Ethan Kolb did it.

Amanda drove Trent to the nearest doctor's office where he was treated and released.

Trent had a great time until Ethan terrorized him and Amanda. Not wanting Ethan Kolb to ruin their first date, he wondered if Amanda wanted to continue.

"Do you want me to drive you back to the mountain?" Amanda asked, thinking that their date was over.

"Yes, we're not done with our date. We will go back to The Knolls and enjoy the rest of the day, the evening, and Sunday morning. Ethan will leave us alone now that he knows he shot me. I will not allow that idiot to ruin this date."

Both of them piled back into her Jeep and drove to where their day had begun. They walked back up to the mountain, continued their date, and stayed the entire weekend.

It was there that he and Amanda had sex for the first time amid the stars, despite his bandaged midsection.

Cuddling afterward, they watched the sun come up as both wondered and hoped that the coming days would be just as wonderful as the previous night had been, with the exception of Ethan shooting him.

After sleeping for a few hours, they decided to go fishing down by the same river where Ethan shot him. She wasn't interested in fishing but she wanted to experience it with Trent.

They didn't care if they caught fish.

They set the lines and propped up the poles and lay together in the soft grass, with Amanda resting her head on his chest and talking about anything that came into her mind, Trent listening intently to every word she said.

She was in mid-sentence when Trent saw that he'd caught a fish and his reel spun very fast.

Manning the pole, he reeled in his catch with Amanda intently looking on to see what he'd caught. A huge bass wriggled on the line and he asked Amanda to unhook it.

"You're joking, right?" She tried to handle the slimy fish.

"Careful with the fins, sweetheart."

He watched her with great delight as the wriggling fish continued to escape her grasp.

"I can't hold it, Trent. It's gross! You do it!" she demanded. She concentrated more on the fact that he called her sweetheart for the first time than on the slimy fish.

"Okay, I'll get it. Do you want me to fry it up?" he asked.

Looking at the struggling fish in Trent's hand, she stated, "No! Trent, let it go. I have lots of food and besides, I don't want anything killed on this trip. Outside of the bear chasing us and you getting shot, it's been so perfect and I don't want to jinx it by having something die."

"Absolutely, Amanda. I'll let it go." Trent smiled and unhooked his wriggling catch.

Smiling broadly, she replied, "Call me sweetheart again. I do so enjoy hearing you call me that."

Trent threw the fish back into the river, embraced her, and kissed her gently for an extended period of time.

The moment was perfect and they kissed more passionately as the river ran past them, not caring what its beauty created on its banks.

The clearing they were in was a perfect place for camping, so they moved their previous camp.

It was Sunday and they didn't want the date to end, so he called his father to ask if he could extend his stay for another day, and his father agreed that he could. They stayed their last night there with the sounds of the running brook and the silence of a billion stars overhead, creating a utopia that both of them wouldn't soon forget.

Trent was usually a quiet man but once he bonded with Amanda, he opened up and always had something to say as she stared into his eyes and listened to every word, just as he had done earlier when she talked wildly about nothing.

The weekend ended, and Trent had a debt to collect from Ethan Kolb. He said goodbye to Amanda and made plans to see her that night.

***

Driving to Ethan Kolb's house with his fully automatic AR-15 rifle and his sidearm in his hip's holster, he sought revenge and compensation.

He spied Ethan's pristine red 1969 Corvette that he loved more than any woman or brother. Trent yelled to the house for Ethan to come out.

Seeing Trent standing in his dirt driveway from his window, he fired a few shots into the air.

Ignoring the shots, Trent demanded, "Ethan Kolb! Get your dumb ass out here!"

Screaming at the house, he pushed a fully loaded magazine into his rifle.

Ethan ran out armed to the teeth. "What the fuck do you want, dickhead?" He pulled up the shoulder strap of his farmer's pants.

"You owe me $585.76, asshole!" Trent angrily demanded. Pointing his rifle at him, he looked down at it and then, back to Ethan. "Yeah, that's right. You've seen this gun before, haven't you? Up on The Knolls. You thought you killed me, didn't you? You know what it can do and you know that I'm not afraid to put one in your idiotic head."

"I ain't giving you shit, asshole!"

Ethan raised his rifle.

"What are you going to do now, chump?" he spouted, angrily.

Pulling his sidearm, Trent shot the rifle out of Ethan's hand with such speed that Ethan didn't have enough time to get off a shot.

Chapter 6
Confronting Ethan

"That's my best rifle, you son of a bitch!"

"I said I want $585.76 and I want it right now." Trent lifted his assault rifle and pointed twenty rounds of destruction at Ethan's prized Corvette.

Ethan looked at his car and then at Trent and angrily stated, "I dare you, asshole!"

Trent fired three rounds through the Corvette's windshield without batting an eye.

"Wait, stop! Goddammit! How do I owe you five hundred dollars?" Ethan removed his wallet from his pocket.

"$400.75 for my windshield you blew out. $175.00 for Doc Miller to sew up my gut, and $10.01 for a new belt. I know you carry a grand with you all the time. The Vette's hood gets the next rounds, you asshole! It'd be a shame to mess up that custom paint job. I will provide it with fifteen or twenty vent holes, though, if I have to ask you again."

"Okay! Okay! Lower the fucking gun, dammit! I got your money."

He reached in his pocket again, fishing for his wallet.

"I'll lower it when you place $585.76 on the hood of my fucking truck and then back the fuck away." He pointed his sidearm at Ethan's head with his automatic rifle still pointed toward the car's hood.

"Okay! Okay! Here, take $600.00. Just don't shoot my fucking car anymore!" he pleaded.

"Goddammit, man, didn't you hear me? I said I wanted $585.76, not six hundred," he corrected. He used his sidearm to shoot out the left front tire.

"Okay! Goddammit, Prichard! Stop shooting my fucking car. Here! Here's your goddamn $585.76. Now, get the fuck off my property! Payback's a bitch, asshole!" he threatened, as Trent slowly walked away from Ethan.

Collecting the money, he walked toward the driver's side of the truck, and got behind the wheel, but turned his truck off and got back out with his rifle, walked over to the Corvette, and blasted fifty holes in the hood, obliterating it.

"I gave you your fucking money, Goddammit! Why the hell did you shoot the fuck out of my car?"

Lowering his rifle, Trent walked back to his truck, placed the gun in it's rack, and looked sternly at Ethan. "Pain and suffering, asshole. You don't have enough money to pay for that!"

Trent drove away with Ethan running into his house to collect his brothers and his arsenal. Trent felt satisfied that he stood up for his rights, but he knew that the Kolbs' desire for revenge was so strong that the confrontation would spark a serious retaliation somewhere down the road. He returned to the store, told his father what he'd done, and warned Ben to expect something from the Kolb's in retaliation.

"I'm proud of you, son. Don't worry about me. None of them will get the better of me. Those red-necks aren't smart enough to do anything but drink and act a fool." Ben patted young Trent on his back and felt a pride that only a father could feel.

***

The memories of those times calmed Trent in his confined space as he thought of ways to extricate himself.

He thought about that first date with Amanda and a hundred of them afterward, as well as father-son interactions with Ben. He even mustered a smile when he thought about his lovely girlfriend trying to wrangle that slimy bass again.

Her expression that day made him smile often.

He also remembered after that special first date, their wedding two years later in the local park. Late August, with seventy-eight degree weather, a gentle breeze, and the aroma of a multitude of flowers marked her path as she slowly walked the lovers' walk toward him to a similarly adorned altar.

That was where they said their vows as mothers cried glorious tears and fathers felt overwhelmed with pride. It was one of the happiest days of his life.

Ethan Kolb continued to terrorize. There were many instances where Ben had caught him doing many nefarious things and each time, Ben foiled his plot and made him not only look as guilty as he proved to be, but made him look foolish in the process. Each time Ben caught him in the act, it enhanced Ethan's desire for revenge.

One cold, snowy morning, the Pritchards drove home from church because two feet of snow blanketed their normal walking path. The roads were treacherously packed with snow and ice but easily passable with Ben's four-wheel drive truck.

Ethan Kolb drove his pickup truck and noticed Prichard's car coming at him.

He purposely drove in their lane as they came around a curve, which sent their car over a cliff, killing them instantly.

Trent opened his eyes at times when he recounted how his parents died in that fiery crash and later finding out how they went off the cliff. In his mind, he could picture the series of events even though he wasn't there to witness them.

Trent assumed Ethan was the culprit but no evidence existed to back up his assertion. He imagined the horror that his parents felt as they tumbled down the ravine to their ultimate demise. He closed his eyes and continued his remembrance, bypassing the incident as much as he could.

Trent and Amanda lived at the store with his parents until the builders finished the construction of their own home.

A day went by, and he reported his parents missing, and he remembered that he and Amanda felt terribly worried. So much so, that they braved the blizzard conditions to search themselves but they couldn't find them.

The dense snow quickly covered the smashed and burned-out car at the bottom of a steep, rocky ravine, so the crime went undiscovered for weeks.

A search party found the car a month later, and authorities removed his parents' remains for burial. The snow eventually melted to reveal the demolished car.

The police called it a tragic accident but Trent immediately knew where the responsibility lay. He had no evidence, but he got word through small-town gossip that Ethan was responsible and he didn't deny it when confronted. The remembrance made Trent angry all over again, thinking back to that time, but his next thought was the one that always brought a smile to his face; later in the thought, it also brought out the madman in him.

It was a quiet night, close to closing time when Amanda informed Trent that he was about to become a father.

Extraordinarily happy, he wanted to treat his wife to an early dinner at one of the nicest restaurants in the adjoining town of Lost River.

He went to his office at the back of the store to count up receipts of the day's sales, while a happy Amanda went to close the doors of the store.

However, before she could lock the door, a drunken Ethan arrived and wanted cartridges for a weekend party he planned.

Drunk and slurring his words, he saw Amanda and said, "Well, don't you look purdy. I'm having a party. Why don't you leave that loser of a husband and come on over. I'll make some room for your sweet ass."

"Fuck you, Ethan! Get the hell out of here. We're closed!"

She attempted to slam the door in his face.

"Closed? You fucking bitch! Do you know who I am? I need some shells. Never mind! Why the hell am I even talking to you? I'll get them myself."

He pushed Amanda aside, barged into the store, and began emptying the shelves and stashing boxes of cartridges into a burlap potato bag.

"No you won't, you son of a bitch. I told you to get the hell out of here! You're drunk and you're armed. We're not going to sell you bullets when you're armed."

She pushed him away from the shelves, spilling the boxes of cartridges on the floor.

"Who said anything about buying them? Now get the fuck out of my way, bitch!" He continued to take what he wanted.

Amanda knocked the two boxes from his hand, and they spilled all over the floor.

Pulling her close to him, she fought the brave fight but he forcibly kissed her, and grabbed her ass.

Trent, hearing the yelling and screaming, ran up the stairs and saw Ethan pummeling Amanda and ripping her clothes off.

"I know you want it! Bitch!"

He mercilessly slugged her unconscious to thwart Amanda's fierce defiance.

Grabbing Ethan with a ferocious rage, Trent flung Ethan like a rag doll against the wall. He ran to Amanda lying on the floor and saw blood coming from the mouth of his unconscious wife. He tried to wake her up.

Meanwhile, Ethan grabbed his pistol and shot Trent in the back.

He fell back behind the counter, but as Ethan approached to finish him off, Trent came up with a shotgun and blasted Ethan in the chest, which sent him sliding across the hardwood floor and crashing into a display case. Trent staggered toward his wife who woke up wondering what had happened.

"Sweetheart, are you okay? Please tell me you're okay!" he pleaded, as he frantically tried to help her.

She responded slowly but noticed something happening.

"Trent! Behind you! Ethan!" she screamed.

Trent, still holding his pistol, shot Ethan again and again and again, but Ethan got one shot off before Trent killed him with the final shot to his head.

Ethan's errant shot caught Amanda in her head and she died, an instant before Ethan hit the floor.

Inconsolable and struggling because of his own injuries, he crawled courageously toward his stilled wife. Gathering Amanda in his arms, he cried profusely as she bled through his fingers. Trent completely forgot that Ethan shot him and severely wounded him as well. He gently laid Amanda down, closed her still-open eyes, and apologized to her for not being there fast enough. He spied a dead Ethan and pumped four more shots into him seemingly to assist in his grief.

Later, after realizing the Ethan can no longer hurt him, he called the fire department and they dispatched an ambulance to the shop.

The police arrived as well to see that Ethan had actually shot Trent twice but he was still conscious as they placed Amanda and Ethan in black body bags. Trent escaped from the paramedics to see Amanda one more time as they closed up the bag, solidifying the image in his mind for his eternity. He collapsed by her side and the paramedics turned him over to see tears still coming from his eyes and blood coming from his nose and mouth.

***

Trent survived his wounds, but was not well enough to attend Amanda's funeral. It was months before the hospital allowed him to leave because his wounds were severe enough to warrant a long stay.

The first thing he did was to visit her grave. He slowly approached the monument and soon he stood in front of it, reading the words her father placed on it.

He brought and placed roses in the small vase attached to it because roses were her favorite flower.

He touched the angels engraved in the smooth marble stone that read:

Amanda Lynn Prichard
Born April 10, 1992 - Died January 15, 2021
Loving wife to Trent Prichard and mother of their unborn son Benjamin Pritchard. Taken from us too soon but supplied us with 28 years of love.

The torturous sight of his beloved wife and son's monument caused him to collapse. Those that found him returned him to the hospital. When he awakened, the doctors excoriated him for leaving the hospital too soon.

It was not too long before the remainder of the Kolb brothers paid a visit to the state police demanding that the authorities arrest Trent for the murder of their eldest brother.

The people of the town laughed at the thought of bringing charges against Trent, and despite Randolph Kolb's money, no lawyer in West Virginia took the case because of the overwhelming evidence that Ethan obviously did the deed and the fact that Trent had lost his wife and unborn son.

During his second hospitalization, the merchants in town took turns opening and closing the Sportsmen store, much to the delight of Trent.

The remaining Kolb brothers vowed to avenge their brother's death, regardless of what Ethan did that fateful night or whom he killed. They tried to intimidate Trent many times over the next few weeks by shooting holes in his store after hours, as well as his truck. Trent knew who attacked and terrorized him but did nothing to prevent it nor did he seek revenge or restitution for the damage.

Trent was not the same man once he returned to the emptiness of his father's store a few weeks later.

There was no more Amanda and no more joy in the grieving man's life. Seven months later, the death of Amanda hit him even harder because it was the time when she was supposed to be giving birth to his son.

He and Amanda never had an opportunity to choose a name for his son but he remembered back to when they were dating, she intimated that she liked his father's name should she ever get pregnant and had a boy.

Since they didn't suggest a name prior to her death, he speculated that she mentioned it to her mother or father and they took it upon themselves to place Benjamin's name on her tombstone, and he had no issue with it.

Chapter 7
A Fateful Meeting

Many women tried to catch his eye in the months that passed. As a single man, he remained true to Amanda because he still loved her and he wouldn't date someone else until that feeling faded with time.

To him, the love he felt for his wife was as strong as ever, so he let the women down easy because that was his way.

The remaining Kolb brothers continued their attacks but waned over time because Trent didn't react to them; they got bored trying to goad him into a fight and eventually stopped.

They came in as customers, and he sold them the cartridges and supplies that they required amid tirades and cursing because his store was the only place within fifty miles that sold what they needed.

Trent calmly rang up their total, demanded payment, and allowed them to leave quietly, despite the expletives and hate they spouted as they walked out the door.

He learned to control his temper when he saw them in his day-to-day travels.

One night at closing time, Trent had a visitor. An old man, whom he didn't recognize and dressed in a suit and a long black coat, slowly walked up to the bench in the corner of the store and sat down amid the nostalgic museum his father had erected for the people of the town.

"Sir, can I help you? We're just about ready to close." Trent walked over to the man with his pad of paper.

"No one can help me. Son, do you know who I am?"

Trent looked at his unfamiliar face and said, "No, sir, I don't think we've met."

"I'm him." He pointed at an old faded photo of his father and his childhood friends.

"You're Patch?" he asked.

"Hell no! That's Patch." He sternly pointed at the photo again. "I'm right there beside your father. I'm Randolph Kolb," the man wistfully informed Trent.

"Mr. Kolb? It's nice to meet you." Trent greeted him and he held out his hand.

Looking at Trent's outstretched hand, Randolph said, "You're definitely Ben's son. Unflinching kindness in the face of the man whose sons have terrorized you and the whole town."

Kolb shook his hand firmly, looked him square in the eye, and stated, "I see Ben in your face. You see, your father used to be my best friend. We did everything together. Even dated the same girl a few times, in our youth. Ah, those were the days of our lives. So free of commitment and allowed to explore on a whim. We were inseparable."

He pointed to the photo on the wall of the five young friends and touched the face of Trent's father and his mother.

Kolb continued, "Did you know that I dated your mother prior to your father marrying her?"

"Yes, I believe my father told me that many years ago."

"An amazing woman! I allowed my job to cloud my love for her and she left me. God, I loved her so, but I knew that Ben would be a good husband and treat her well. He dedicated this whole wall to five young boys. The time of our lives."

"How can I help you, Mr. Kolb?"

"I came to offer my condolences for your losses and to apologize for all that my sons have done to you and your family. I have no control over them anymore. I don't give them money, they steal it, and I have sustained many beatings over the years because of my reluctance to agree with what they do. I am a prisoner in my own home. I come here tonight to tell you how much your father and mother meant to me. I saw you at your wife's grave earlier today. I visited there for my eldest who they buried in the same cemetery. Regardless of how he conducted his life, he was still my son." The man lamented and continued.

"I wanted to talk to you but you were already having a conversation with your deceased wife and I didn't have the heart to interrupt such a beautiful soliloquy. You speak to her as if she stood right in front of you. I liked that."

Trent confessed, "I loved her more than life."

Kolb continued, "While I visited the cemetery, I saw the graves of your parents and I cried because the adventures we had together, as children, are still so vivid in my memory. We had big plans as children. Patch dated a girl from New Jersey and later, after he died, I married her. Now Remy and I are the only ones left and I feel that I needed to talk to you before I pass on because I feel that it will happen soon."

"I appreciate your sentiments, Mr. Kolb. I don't blame you for the death of my family. I know that because my father used to be quite fond of you as well and had the same thoughts of his youth and his friendship with you. You have done great things for this town and state."

Helping the old man to his feet, Trent stated. "I thank you for dropping by and hope that your sons don't find out that you visited. Is that all you wanted to say?"

"No! The real reason why I'm here is to inform you that you, not my sons, will inherit all my wealth and properties. I owe it to Ben, Remy, Jordy, and all the rest for allowing me to keep the memories of such a special time," Kolb confessed.

"That's very generous of you, Mr. Kolb." Trent happily shook the old man's hand again.

"Well, I have to go but I have one request," Kolb stated.

"Sure, anything."

"May I take this photo? We took this at Glover's pond and it represents a time when I smiled most of the time." He pointed to the photo of the five friends by the pond.

Reaching over on the wall, Trent pulled the old framed photo down, and said, "Sure, Mr. Kolb. Here, take it. I'm sure that my father would've loved to have given it to you himself."

"I know he would have, knowing his generous nature. I really wish I saw him more often after he married Margie, but I guess I remained a stubbornly jealous old man. I'd have quit my job in a heartbeat knowing what I know now."

Kolb sighed as Trent handed him the photo. "Thank you, son. I will look at this when I feel my time is at hand. This is the last memory I want to take with me from this life," Kolb sadly stated, as a tear flowed down his wrinkled face.

Kolb left that night and Trent never saw him again. He thought about the old man often and wondered how a kind and generous man like Randolph Kolb could have had sons who seemed like the spawn of the devil himself.

Amazed and bewildered at the demeanor of the elder Kolb. Trent admitted, to himself, that his past thoughts about the man were wrong and felt very pleased to have had the opportunity to talk to him.

***

Days went by and Trent visited the gravesite every day as usual, and each time he saw Amanda's monument, he got angrier.

Later, he found out what the Kolb brothers had planned for their afternoon. They followed him to the cemetery. Trent walked up to his precious wife's tombstone as usual, but saw a horrific sight. Someone had knocked it over and broken it into four large pieces.

Trent, appalled at what he saw, attempted to right the stones when he saw the four Kolb brothers emerge from behind the larger monuments and walk toward him.

"What the hell? I knew you guys were responsible for this. So, which one wants his beating first? I will fuck up all four of you!" Trent angrily announced, as the rage in him built up to its peak.

"You ain't going to do shit, Pritchard!"

Wyatt motioned to one of their friends who hid behind a monument to his rear. He hit Trent on the back of the head, rendering him unconscious and bleeding from his head. The Kolb brothers gathered up Trent and carried him away from the cemetery. The blow to his head caused a short-term memory loss, and he only remembered walking up to Amanda's grave.

***

That was the last memory he had prior to his incarceration. He wished he had more happy memories, because the happier ones calmed him, but the evil ones incensed him and calm was the emotion he needed to get out of his predicament.

Using his thoughts of Amanda to gather enough strength to fight back, he realized that he might just survive his ordeal. He had to reduce his heart rate because the claustrophobic nature of his reality sped it up to scary levels once again. Due to the silence of his prison, he heard how fast it got.

The memory of seeing his beautiful wife lying slaughtered on the floor caused him to unconsciously react violently within the box.

A surge of adrenaline came to him when he remembered his wife's toppled monument, but what really gave him strength beyond measure was an assumption of what his son's face would've looked like had he had the chance to grow up.

Kicking violently at the back of the box, as if God himself assisted him, it exploded out and away from the box and into an empty chasm within the grave.

He screamed, "Holy shit!"

Realized that they'd dug the hole too big, a large void existed at the back and underneath half of the box. Dirt from above poured inside the hastily made box by his feet. He simply pushed it into the void.

The more the box filled up, the more he pushed out. Soon, the dirt piled atop his pine coffin, lessened. He twisted his body around with hopes of using his hands to bring more dirt into the box but he couldn't. He found the beer cans and used his knife to cut the cans into makeshift spoons.

He cracked and removed one of the thin planks on top of the box that spanned the length of it, used the cans to spoon dirt into the box, and then he simply pushed the dirt to his feet and kicked it into the open space.

Water came through the dirt and he knew that it appeared to be raining, which also compacted the soil, making it settle.

He was happy that he still had the PVC pipes to supply him with enough air to allow him to exert the amount of energy necessary to dig himself out of his dark space.

Soon, dirt turned to mud, which made it harder for him to push it out but the water made the void larger and created more space to place the mud.

Eventually, the space at his feet filled in but the amount of dirt on top of him was only a few inches thick. He pushed his arm through and he felt that he just had a few inches of soil left to spoon out before he freed himself.

An hour of digging later, he found that the capacity of the box that he was buried in was about to be maxed out with regard to space, so for the last two inches he had to hold his breath and make a final stab at getting his head above ground and breathe fresh air again.

Removing the last two planks, which were the only things left that covered the box, he struggled to remove the rest of the dirt and mud which flooded in the box and eventually, filled it completely. Holding his breath, he stabbed at the mud and dirt trying to get his head through the muck.

Struggle as he may, he ran out of air and made a final desperate push through the mud.

His head blasted through what was left of his grave from the top of his head to right below his nose, and he gasped to gather air. He freed himself to his neck but the mud was heavy. Though he was weak, he struggled mightily to free both arms.

Wiping his eyes, he opened them to see the nighttime sky and torrential rain washing the mud from his face. A lightning strike lit up the area and he noticed during the brief brightly lit sky that he was in a thick forest that he didn't recognize.

Weak from his struggle, he paused with just his torso above ground as he gained strength to make the final push to completely free himself.

With his energy spent, every muscle in his body stretched and ached badly. An hour later, he gradually pushed himself up to free himself to his hips, then had to wait until he had enough feeling in his legs to complete his freedom from his grave.

His thoughts gave him strength to persevere and save himself, and his painful memories supplied him with enough rage to propel him to completely and miraculously free himself.

Finally, after hours of painful struggle, he was completely out of his dark box. Muddied, wet, and free, he laid beside his grave thankful for his remembrances. Rain bounced off his face, rinsing away much of the mud. He couldn't move so he rested there wondering what he'd do to the Kolb brothers once he regained his strength.

As much as he wanted to lie down and sleep, he moved away from the grave in case the kidnappers returned and sent him back to his prison. Strangely, he thought he should be starving and dehydrated, not having eaten or drunk anything for at least a day. He had no idea how long the whole ordeal had taken.

He thought that the reason he wasn't hungry or thirsty was because the fear and adrenaline predominantly fueled his mind and that clouded any thoughts of sustenance.

Trent crawled into the brush and hid among the undergrowth of the forest. The torrential rain pelted him but his hiding place blocked much of it.

It was there where he was finally able to sleep among the trees instead of dirt peppering down on his face.

Under recent circumstances, his environment, his mud-laden clothes, as well as his injuries, might have prevented his ability to sleep but his body was so spent, it didn't matter where he was or the extent of his injuries; he wasn't going to take another step or crawl another inch until he gathered some sleep. Safely away from his grave, he smiled for the first time, realizing that he really didn't feel as tired as he thought. He still laid down and eventually fell asleep.

Waking up the next day, he felt fully refreshed.

The torrential downfall cleaned his face and much of the mud from him during the night, although he didn't remember whether or not he even closed his eyes.

A bright sun baked what little was left of the mud onto his face and body. Blinking his eyes, he remained there trying to determine where his injuries, if any, were. Moving his arms and legs, he sat up and stretched his muscles. The mud, which caked his clothes, cracked as the sun bore down on him.

Surprisingly, he felt no pain and attempted to stand up. The absence of pain masked the fact that his legs still felt weak; he fell back hard to the ground, then sat up and leaned against a nearby tree. He wasn't aware of where he was, which surprised him because he thought that he'd spent a lifetime surveying all the forests surrounding his hometown.

Chapter 8
The Reckoning

What am I to do now? he wondered to himself. I can't go to the authorities because the Kolb family owns the local sheriff's office, and their father will just get them off with a small fine, he further thought.

However, after his late-night talk with Randolph Kolb, he wondered whether he actually would bail them out. He'd visited Ethan's grave so it appeared that, regardless of his sons' transgressions, he still cared for them.

Trent wanted his kidnappers to believe that he remained buried in his makeshift coffin, because he couldn't run from them, should they find out that he'd escaped. Backtracking to where they buried him, it shocked him to see that it was just a few feet away when he'd spent hours walking away from it.

Seeing shovels left behind by his kidnappers, he straightened out the grave, replaced the two PVC pipes to where he thought they were originally, and saw to it that the fan still worked. He sensed an uneasy feeling being at the grave and quickly moved away from it.

Obviously, he didn't know exactly what the grave looked like while he dwelled within it, but he did what he could to rebuild it until the feeling hit him. He carefully placed the shovels exactly where he found them.

With his strength returning to normal, he took a walk through the woods, hoping that something he saw sparked a remembrance as to where he was so he could determine how to get home. Then, he'd decide what to do about his kidnapping. Encountering a small babbling creek, he looked at his clothes. The caked-on mud was a burden to him, so he jumped in, sloshing around as the clear fresh water turned brown and cloudy with every motion. Dipping his head below the surface, he rinsed the rest of the mud from his face and hair, and afterward, felt completely refreshed as his clothes dried quickly in the midday sun. He had an idea as to how to deal with the Kolb family once and for all.

He'd spent a lifetime watching the Kolbs terrorize the town as well as him and his family personally.

He assumed he was, to them, dead or buried and near dead, which presented a unique opportunity for him to do the terrorizing for once.

He struggled between wanting to get back to his life and teaching the Kolb brothers a lesson they wouldn't soon forget.

What kind of life am I returning to? he asked himself.

He was a mere storekeeper who bided his time until boredom and old age sapped what life had left to offer.

His loving parents and the love of his life were gone, and with Amanda, his unborn child. Hopes of an equally happy life with someone else seemed impossible, because of the horrible visions of the blood of his deceased wife streaming through his fingers as he held her head in his hands. A destructive memory that overruled any happy thought of a better day.

Conflicted as to what to do, he walked back to the grave and saw that his kidnappers had returned to their captive in the forest and left again. They were long gone when he arrived, but he saw that they pulled the two PVC pipes out of the ground, and took them and the shovels with them. They gave their perceived captive an unspeakably cruel death by suffocation, hiding their crime forever. Or, so they thought. It was then that he formulated his plan for the Kolb brothers.

If his plan worked, then the Kolb brothers would see things that would haunt them forever, and maybe drive them to church the following Sunday as Remy wished they would.

Trent's plan was to haunt them relentlessly. He'd appear before them as a ghost and make them either turn themselves in or put a bullet in their brain.

Trent wanted the latter to happen more than the former, but later realized that a simple bullet to the brain would be too quick for all the pain and havoc that they'd created in his short lifetime. First, he had to find out where he was to set his plan in motion.

Walking what he thought was west, he hoped something he saw as a child or a young adult, might spark a memory. He walked for hours as the sun set and still, there was nothing he remembered.

Hours later, darkness replaced the bright sunshine, but he kept walking through the thicket with just fireflies supplying flickers of light in the deep, dark forest. He remembered where his flashlight was but there wasn't a chance in hell that he'd return to his past grave and dig it up with a slim hope that it still worked. His pocketknife also was lost in that place. Devoid of those two important tools, he now just depended on his survival skills and his wits to get him through the seemingly never-ending forest.

Climbing to higher ground to survey the forest, in the distance, he spied what appeared to be a campfire in a clearing about a half-mile walk from where he was. Surprised that after all he'd gone through up to this point hadn't seemed to affect him physically, he felt full of energy and strangely, never seemed to tire.

His resolve to see things righted was his reasoning for the seemingly spry and energetic walk toward the campsite.

Cautious about entering another man's campsite in the dead of night, he didn't want to startle the campers into raising a gun toward the sounds he made.

Intruders who make noises in the dead calm of the forest are often accidentally shot and killed. He noticed where his feet landed in order not to snap a branch or rustle the leaves to startle whoever lit the fire.

Approaching the campsite, he spied an old man sitting in front of the flickering fire warming a kettle. Dressed in a fur hat and wearing a homemade leather outfit, Trent felt like the man was approachable. Obviously, he was a man who'd been in the woods for a long time, because his rudimentary thatch roof lean-to appeared so old that new grass grew from it. His clothes were made of animal skins, carefully and expertly stitched together. The man's worn boots looked as if they'd traveled many roads and unseen paths.

His long beard and weathered face also gave Trent a clue that the woods were not merely a weekend excursion, but his home. Trent hailed the man but his sudden words didn't startle him at all; he continued minding his kettle.

A lone mule milled about near a wooden cart, indicating the man's only mode of transport.

"Come ahead." The old man stood up with a broad smile on his face. "Don't be scared, lad, come ahead."

Trent nervously approached the old man's camp.

"Welcome, son. O'Flaherty's my name. Who are you?"

Trent walked toward him, still cautious as to who he was and why he appeared to be living in the woods.

"Pritchard, Trent Prichard. I saw your fire from the distance. I'm lost."

"Well, you're not lost anymore, Trent. Come on over and sit by the fire. I have seen very few people over the years,"

The old man cleared a spot on the log he sat on.

Cautious, Trent sat down on an old nearby cooler, with broken handles, near the log. "Do you live out here all by yourself?"

"Yes, I've not the patience for the people in towns and cities. I've seen and lived in many of them, and when my time came, I decided that it's out here that still makes me wonder as a child wonders. Life never gets old out here. This forest provides me with everything I need. I love to discover new things, and things that I've never seen before are all around me. I think that new discovery is why we all search. To find things that amaze us and in this place, I see new things all the time," the man said, with a decisiveness that made Trent believe that the old man was an educated man who'd seen too much of civilization.

"That's a very nice outlook. I've never thought about that before. How long have you been out here?"

"Lost track of time years ago. I've stopped caring about time and its ramifications. Now, I just take it as it comes. I told you that I see new things all the time and you are a perfect example of that, Trent. Why are you out here?" He placed another log on the fire.

"It's a long, sad story, sir. Do you have a first name?"

"Been a long time since I used my given name or even thought about it. My old Irish father always taught me that my last name held more importance than any other name. My mother called me Elijah but you can call me Eli if that makes it easier for you. What's the long story?" he asked, eager to hear another's tale.

"Well, a gang of brothers who tortured and terrorized my small community for years, kidnapped me. They were responsible for my parents' deaths, as well as my wife and child's. They buried me alive about a mile from here hoping to torture me into telling them where my father stashed all his money, but I didn't tell them. I escaped the grave and have been walking aimlessly trying to find out where I am ever since." Tears welled up as he recounted all that he had lost in the last few years.

"I bet you're talking about the Kolb brothers, right?"

Trent's eyes widened because the man seemed to know someone he knew. "Yes, that's right. You've heard of them?"

The old man stood up and placed another log on the fire; it crackled and instantly the fire engulfed it. Orange embers floated up brightening the dark sky.

"Yes, I've seen them in these woods many times. I've watched them as they randomly shoot the animals and laugh while watching for their last breath. They are a cruel bunch but they'll not see what we see out here," he said with a calm, reassuring voice.

"That's them, all right," assured Trent.

The man looked up to Trent and said, "They are a vile bunch. Yes. That they are."

Trent continued, "Well, I've never been a man who sought revenge. I've always allowed people to be what they are, but I snapped when I saw that they cruelly pulled the air supply from where they buried me, wanting me to die that way."

"Any sane man should have snapped at the death of their loved ones. Why did it take you so long?" the old man wondered.

It appeared to Trent that he was more interested in Trent's story than in whatever he cooked in the kettle.

"I don't know. I think that I died that day holding my wife in my arms. Life held no meaning after that and I gave up trying to be happy. Now, I've got the right perspective, and I see what they've taken from me. I can't bring back my wife and child, but I can take back my soul." The first trickle of a tear streamed down his weary face.

"Ah yes, the soul is a very important possession that we all must protect. We can't see or touch it but we know its's there. It's reserved for times when sorrowful events are most dire. It's what makes us believe that hope will prevail regardless of the losses we endure and the only thing we have left when we die. It tracks the roads we've walked on during our time and allows others to remember that we were once among them."

"Are you a philosopher, Eli, because you speak as if you've already lived through every facet of life?"

"These old bones have seen my share of despair. Life and death are merely a means to a beginning or an end. It's what we do in the middle that marks our existence and then allows for further exploration beyond the limits of knowledge. In other words, you are judged by what you've done, and should a higher power see your deeds with favor, he'll allow you to see the true meaning as to why you were born."

The old man smiled broadly and his profound words resonated with young Trent.

Trent looked at the man in amazement as he clearly, and distinctly, created a plausible scenario within his mind as to why all the good and bad happened to him. However, he wondered whether or not the powers that be would continue to see him in such a glorious light, should he carry out his plan with regard to the Kolb brothers.

Chapter 9
Trent Begins

"I like the way you think, Eli. I'm wondering whether or not I should seek revenge on the Kolb brothers now."

Picking up a stone, Trent hurled it into the darkened nearby brush.

"Revenge? I don't look at it like that. I feel that you're ridding the world of evil. The stone that you just threw—do you expect it to be hurled back at you?" he asked rhetorically. "No, of course you don't. If someone always throws the stone back, eventually you'll stop throwing them. They are young men who throw stones constantly and will continue to terrorize many a good people for many years to come, if you don't start throwing stones back. I see it as doing humanity a great service and, if I may be so bold, I'd like to help you."

The old man stoked the fire further and the flames rose dramatically.

"I understand your thinking and you're right! I could certainly use the help. Here's what I want to do."

Trent spent the next five hours explaining his plan, and Eli eagerly listened and agreed with it all. First, Eli showed Trent where he was because he had to make a visit to his shop to prepare for a long adventure; the destruction of the remaining four brothers who cared little about the people around them.

He realized that he was just a mile away from his shop, which amazed him because he thought that he knew the woods surrounding his store like the back of his hand.

Together, they trekked through the thick woods and walked toward Trent's Sportsmen's store. He and Eli went to the back of the store and broke a window. Trent climbed in and saw that the Kolb brothers completely tore his store and home apart looking for the hidden cash.

"Wow, they even tore off the drywall from the walls," he said of their search of his father's secret hiding place.

"I guess they didn't find it, Trent. Your father must have hidden it well."

"Oh, he did, but we don't need that."

Trent knew of the safe, and where his father hid it, but saw that they hadn't come close to finding it. Trent didn't need money, so he left it where it was, but he gathered up a few rifles and lots of ammunition.

Locating a large package in the back of the store that a production company purchased for a film that they were going to make a year earlier, he collected it.

The film never materialized, and Ben got stuck with two cases of blank shells for multiple types of firearms. He handed them out the window to Eli, who placed them on his handmade mule-cart designed for travel in the woods. He also handed out a few camping accessories that he thought Eli could use.

"We don't need these supplies, Trent. The woods provide us shelter and a great hiding place. We have the stars to guide us and a bright moon to supply us light." Eli loaded it all on his cart anyway.

"You're probably right, but we'll have them if we need them."

Trent looked around for anything that could assist them.

He spied the spare set of keys to his truck, but realized that where they were going preempted the need for a truck, and left the keys on its hook. He climbed back out of the window but he noticed something very strange and unexplainable.

After climbing down from the window and had inventoried everything on the cart, he looked back up to the window and saw that the window was closed and not broken.

"I thought that I broke the window," he said to Eli.

"Nope, you opened the window when we got here. You told me that you always left it unlocked in case you forgot your keys. Don't you remember?"

"No, I remember that I wrapped that old towel around my hand and broke it!"

"No, Trent. We came upon it and you simply opened it. There's no glass on the ground anywhere." Eli pointed to the ground.

"Of course, I'm so fixated on getting this stuff out and not being seen that I completely forgot how I got in. I think we have everything. Let's go to your camp. I think I know where it is now," he stated, as they left the back of the store. Trent still looked at the closed window as the mule guided the cart away.

The two men and the mule cart entered the woods with no one seeing them. Trent felt that they wouldn't encounter anyone during their long trek back to the campsite.

An hour later, they arrived to see that the fire still smoldered and ignited back to its former glory with just a few pokes by a makeshift poker and two or three more logs. The two conspirators finalized their plan.

***

They felt no need to hurry to carry out their plan, because they had all the time in the world to start. They walked past the forest Trent used to walk through and ventured farther into unfamiliar woods. They set out to explore.

Noticing wildlife frolicking amid beautiful meadows free from worry of hunters, he allowed them to pass by even though he had them square in his sights.

The animals seemed different in those parts of the woods, as they appeared to be unafraid of either of them.

Trent thought that during the decades Eli lived in the forest, he'd created a sanctuary for the animals, since they approached him to get a small morsel of food consisting mostly of bread and berries. Trent laid back and watched in astonishment at Eli's extraordinary interaction with the animals. Even the fiercest of beasts bowed to the generosity of the mountain man. Eli didn't own a rifle or any means to defend himself because, as he put it, the animals protected him from harm and provided the needed comradeship in the wild that he missed as a youth in nearby bustling towns.

The simplistic nature of the man intrigued Trent, and his ease of mind was something that he hoped that he could mimic one day.

The desire to enact his revenge was still first and foremost on his mind, but the travels with Eli made Trent realize that there was a big world out there for anyone who possessed the desire to see it for its worth. The trees of the forest weren't merely trees to Eli; they were his reason for his existence and the animals were equally important as they represented his family.

Eli hadn't the heart to harm any of them, regardless of what they'd provided for Trent and his ilk in the past.

For reasons that escaped him, Trent no longer cared that much for the outside world or the trappings of civilized society, but he did miss many of his friends.

***

Weeks later, Trent decided to visit the small town that used to be his sanctuary from his lonely store.

He remembered happier times at his father's store, but since he'd lost so much, it proved to be a prison of sorts.

Walking down the town's only road, he noticed that everything appeared normal. He saw no missing person signs or any acknowledgement of his disappearance on telephone poles or flyers in store windows.

The people seemed different in that no one acknowledged his waves to them on the main street.

Entering the Balls Bluff Tavern. He expected a grand welcome, but there were many new people there he didn't recognize.

Trying to gather Nancy's attention but she, too, ignored him. He walked out not getting served, then noticed an errant newspaper blowing on the ground and saw why. The Kolb brothers saw to it that he'd not be welcomed in town. They planted a story that painted Trent and his family as terrorists who didn't really die.

The story told of a foreign government that planted the family in the tiny town six decades earlier to create a home base for other terrorist to come to and train beyond the sight and knowledge of the United States Government. Then the Kolb brothers took over the Sportsmen store through a court decision.

Heartbroken that the town he had grown up in had turned against him and his family, he continued reading that Randolph Kolb, the Kolb brothers' father, found out about the plot and foiled it before it took shape. The outrageously false story still didn't solve the issue of why they ignored his presence until he happened upon a mirrored surface.

Glancing at himself in the mirror, he saw a different man than he knew. He hadn't shaved in weeks, but the length of his beard seemed to indicate that he had been away much longer than he originally thought.

He had various scars, and even he had a hard time recognizing his own face. It appeared lined with age, his beard sprinkled with wisps of gray.

How long have I been away? he wondered.

Disheartened and confused, he began his trek back to the camp.

Leaving the town, he noticed Morgan Kolb's truck pull into the Balls Bluff Tavern's parking lot. He was curious as to what Morgan would do if he saw him alive and well, so he returned to the tavern.

Morgan walked into the busy bar. The patrons stopped talking and moved away from wherever he sat.

Demanding a beer, he grabbed it out of Nancy's hand before she had a chance to open it. Morgan had turned into Ethan before Trent's eyes. He boldly sat next to Morgan while Nancy walked back to the kitchen.

"What the fuck are you looking at, old man?" he asked as he glared at Trent.

"You, you son of a bitch. You don't remember me, do you?" Trent barked.

"Why should I remember you?" Morgan asked.

Trent banged his hand on the bar and stated, "You should know who I am. I'm Trent Pritchard!"

Morgan laughed and yelled, "Bullshit! He died years ago."

Morgan didn't know it but during the heated exchange, Trent cut his belt from behind, then smacked him so hard he fell backward, hitting his head on the floor. No one saw what Trent had done, and he quickly removed his pants and underwear as he lay stupefied on the floor.

Waking up, Morgan wondered why he was on the floor, and sat back down on his barstool looking around for Trent, but he was gone.

Nancy returned to the bar and Morgan asked her, "Did you see that old dude who sat next to me?"

"Who'd want to sit next to you, asshole? No, there isn't anyone there," Nancy explained, as she cleaned the bar around Morgan.

"Fuck you, Nancy!" Morgan reached behind the bar and grabbed another beer from the cooler. "He said he was Trent Pritchard. I saw him. He sat right there."

"I thought you said that Trent Pritchard was dead or banished from the country?" she asked, accusingly.

"He's dead, dammit!" he said to himself as he drank the entire beer in one long gulp.

"Well, dumbass, if he's dead, how could he have been sitting next to you? Maybe his ghost is coming back to get you Kolbs. I know I would!" She smiled and returned to her duties behind the bar.

Grabbing another beer from the bar's cooler, Nancy demanded, "You have to pay for those, Morgan! I'm getting tired of you and your fucked up brothers stealing me blind."

"As I said, fuck you, Nancy! I'll take what I want and there's not a goddamn thing you can do about it." Morgan opened his beer and guzzled it down.

"Just like your fucking brother," she said, as she turned and walked away but counting how many beers, Morgan consumed.

"Don't you say a goddamn thing about Ethan, bitch!" He threw his half-full beer can at Nancy, hitting her in the head.

Crashing to the floor, many of the patrons came to Nancy's defense, much as they did when Ethan used the same tactics to get out of the bar without paying a dime. Three men stood behind Morgan, then started laughing and pointing at him.

"What the fuck are you guys laughing at? I will kick all your asses!" Morgan stood up as his beer belly flopped below. His belly was so big that he couldn't see that he was completely naked from the waist down.

"We ain't seeing nothing but we're not looking. That table of women over there has a better view of your naked fat ass," they informed Morgan, as they pointed toward the table of giggling women.

The women, seeing what Morgan did to Nancy, ridiculed his tiny package as he searched around for his pants.

"Look at that little thing. No wonder the girls call you dickless." They pointed at his very small appendage and laughed heartily at him.

Humiliated, Morgan tried to cover himself up with his beer bottle but that only made the group of women laugh harder.

Chapter 10
Morgan's Event

The prettiest of the woman came up to Morgan, gave him a lemon slice and said, "That beer bottle is a little overkill, Morgan; here, this will do as well," she said, laughing.

Walking back to her table, she wiggled her pinky finger indicating the length of his member close up.

Morgan scrambled out of the bar, red-faced and humiliated. He got in his truck and found that it didn't start without the coil that Trent removed as he left. Morgan called Everett and told him to bring a pair of pants to the tavern.

"How did you lose your fucking pants, Morgan?" asked Everett.

"Never mind how, dumbass! Just bring them."

"On my way, bro."

Trent called the local fire department, sheriff's office, and the small press and told them that Morgan Kolb had a bomb in his truck.

The police had many more deputies than Trent remembered and they all descended on Morgan's truck with guns drawn and demanded that he get out.

"Get out of the truck, Kolb!" Their guns pointed directly at him.

"I got no pants, goddammit!"

"I said, get out of the fucking truck!" the sheriff demanded. Morgan finally complied. They handcuffed him and placed him in the back of one of the squad cars.

Everett drove up fifteen minutes later with a pair of pants.

He saw Morgan in the back of a squad car, and barked, "What the fuck are you doing, cop? My father will hear of this. What did you do with my brother's pants?"

The sheriff answered with a definitive smirk on his face, "We didn't do anything with his pants. He was naked when we got here. You can take his pants to him over there in the back of the squad car. Let me see them first. I have to check them out for guns. Up against the patrol car, Kolb. I have to pat you down before you approach that idiot."

Everett complied and the cop patted him down but found nothing.

"You're free to go."

"Why are you tearing my brother's truck apart?"

"We got a tip that there is a bomb in it and we're trying to find it. Step away, Everett," the sheriff demanded.

Walking over to the squad car, Everett handed Morgan his pants, and he stepped out of the car and put them on.

"What the fuck is going on, Morgan?"

"I saw him in the bar!" Morgan stated.

"You saw who in the bar?"

"Pritchard sat in the bar. He did something to me and took my pants."

"Bullshit, he's gone. He can't come back. Did anyone else see him?"

Morgan continued, "No! No one saw him. It's like he is a ghost or something."

"Listen, Pritchard's dead. It couldn't have been him," he replied.

He and Morgan left as the police ripped his truck apart.

"I expect you idiots to put my truck back together when you're done, dammit!" Morgan yelled at the sheriff as they pulled away.

Morgan asked Everett, "How the hell do you know that Pritchard's dead?"

"Just going on what I've heard in town, besides we're supposed to stick to the story that we told to the press."

"Never mind. I just want to get home and forget this shit!" Morgan spouted.

It was obvious that Trent couldn't return to town because if they knew who he was, the locals would possibly kill him, knowing how patriotic the citizens of the town were.

Trent had thrown the first stone in his war with the Kolb brothers but he was concerned about the way he looked.

He was certain that it had only been weeks since he extracted himself from the grave, yet he looked as if he's aged twenty years. He meandered back into the camp and met Eli.

"Did you enjoy your walk, Trent?"

"Yes, I did, especially when I heard the sirens. I saw Morgan Kolb in town and started the plan. Eli, how long have I been here?"

Eli looked at his bare arm as if he had a watch on it and said, "How do I know? I don't measure things in terms of time."

Trent knew of Eli's penchant to discard time as a viable measurement.

Forgetting about his looks, he told him that they should visit the Kolbs' home, because he enjoyed watching Morgan in distress and wanted to extend the same punishment to the rest of them.

Eli agreed, but they had a few hours to kill so Eli collected a few dead animals and needed to get them skinned.

Trent, having had plenty of experience as a hunter, happily helped because Eli said that the animals died to make clothes for forest living for him; he had long since worn out the clothes he'd had.

"I thought that you didn't kill animals. Where did these hides come from?" Trent asked.

"They died in the woods. I didn't kill them. They give to me what they can," Eli stated.

He gave the hides to Eli, who sewed them up and created a full leather outfit for him in no time flat. It fit Trent perfectly.

The two men were ready to go to the Kolb house. It was only a mile away, and they set out on foot.

Trent was proud of his new clothes; they made him feel part of the forest, and the craftsmanship was superior to anything he'd ever worn.

They made better time because the thicket didn't leave scratches on his once-exposed skin now protected by the tough leather. Trent brought his rifle and the blank cartridges that he'd gotten from his store.

Trent was aware of all the guns that the Kolbs possessed, because he'd sold them to them.

Eli carried no guns and mocked Trent for his arsenal as they stealthily walked toward the property. They arrived sooner than Trent expected and saw all the brothers drinking by the bonfire with four other friends, and a multitude of young minor girls prancing in various forms of undress.

The first thing he did seemed minor in scope but Trent wanted to do it. He spied Ethan's fully repaired Corvette. He assumed that the car went to Morgan, being the next oldest brother.

He let the air out of the tires. After that, he walked behind the house and fired three shots from his pistol into the back window of the car.

"What the hell is that?" asked one of the men whom Trent didn't know.

"I don't know. Did you accidentally fire one off?" asked Wyatt.

"No, I'd know if I did that. I'm not that fucking drunk."

Wyatt asked, "Bubba, you're so drunk, how could you know? Have another beer and watch these bitches act like fools."

Bubba smiled and said, "I got that one called Brittany. I drugged her beer. She should be out soon and I'll nail her ass good."

"Ha ha, I already had that, Bubba. I'd rather them be awake when I screw them."

"Hell, I don't give a shit if they're awake or dead knocked out. At least I'll get mine," the man said, with a loud laugh and a thorough disregard for the girl's well-being.

Trent heard what he said and knew that the idiots hanging around the Kolbs were just as despicable as the brothers were, and he cared not what happened to Bubba or any of them.

Trent and Eli didn't care if one of their stray bullets landed in Bubba's head.

Brittany, the young daughter of a prominent family within the town, had passed out drunk and drugged on a lawn chair. Her friends tried to awaken her.

Thinking that she was just drunk, they allowed her to sleep it off and ignored her as the other girls playfully pinched each other's breasts to the delight of the older men. The girls danced to the blasting country music that surrounded the house and playfully undressed each other.

Bubba, seeing that the other girls were not paying attention to the knocked-out Brittany, slung her over his shoulder and took her inside the house.

Wyatt, watching Bubba carry Brittany, held his beer up as a toast to what was about to happen and laughed at Bubba's desire to have sex with an unconscious young girl.

Trent followed Bubba into the house and into one of the bedrooms. It was dark, so hiding was easy.

As Bubba ripped her clothes completely off, she awakened and was met with a backhand across her face, knocking her out once again. The cruelty displayed disgusted Trent and Eli, and they prepared to make an example of the ugly drunk. He pulled his pants down and got on top of the helpless girl. Rearing up from the corner he hid in, Trent pistol beat him in the head. The blow didn't kill him but he wanted it to.

However, he did something that proved to be worse than a quick painless death. Bubba sprawled naked on the floor holding his head and cursing at whoever hit him. Opening his eyes, he saw Trent holding a huge knife and walking toward him.

"Who the fuck are you, old man?" he asked, as Trent moved closer.

"I'm the cutter. I come for disgusting guys who kidnap and molest children," Trent angrily explained.

Rearing up, Bubba punched Trent, but the blow missed him.

Seeing the punch thrown with such clarity, he easily avoided it with such skill that Bubba thought the punch went right through him. Dumbfounded, Bubba imagined he saw Trent disappear and reappear as he continued walking toward him.

"What are you?" Bubba asked, as he crawled backward.

"I'm the guy who will prevent you from ever molesting a child or anyone again, and there's not a fucking thing you can do about it. In fact, I'm going to make you do the deed."

Trent threw the knife toward Bubba's hand and it stuck solidly on the hard wood floor right between his legs.

Grabbing the knife, he tried to throw it aside but it didn't leave his hand.

The horror on his face was evident as his knife-wielding right hand reached down and with his left hand stretching out his testicles, slashing them off.

Trent stood back in shock at what Bubba did all by himself. Bubba was too scared to scream, and because he cut them off so quickly, the pain had not reached his nervous system but when it did, he yelped like a wolf in a bear trap, holding his crotch hoping that he didn't do what he thought he'd done.

Dropping the knife, it bounced right back to Trent's hand. Leaning down to the man holding his crotch, Trent smiled, and said, "My, I bet that hurt! Eli, come in here! Look! Bubba cut his balls off!"

Trent wanted to give the knife to Bubba because he wanted to fight him badly, but Bubba held onto his crotch and was in no mood for putting up a good fight as blood squeezed through his fingers. Trent gave the knife to him to mock the futility of him beating Trent, but something happened that Trent didn't understand.

Bubba had castrated himself and appeared to do it because Trent willed him to do it. Trent did nothing but give him the knife and it appeared to Trent, that the knife had a mind of its own.

Eli, who came in through the window, looked at the unconscious girl, and asked, "How old do you think that little girl is?"

"I bet she's fifteen, tops," Trent said.

"That child has a mom and a dad. She has to live with this her entire life. I say that he hasn't paid enough," Eli stated.

Being the experienced mountain man he was, Eli wasn't squeamish with regard to neutering animals, so he waved his hand which removed Bubba's hands from his crotch and Trent watched as Eli cut his penis off as well.

In sheer horror, the man saw his manhood removed quickly. Bubba stood up and frantically ran out to the bonfire naked and holding his crotch.

He bled to death right there in the front yard, with the Kolb brothers and the other men wondering what happened to him.

Neither Trent nor Eli felt the slightest bit guilty for what they'd done. They put the girl's clothes back on and carried her away from the party. She had an ID in her jeans and Trent told Eli that he was going to take her home. They didn't want her to wake up in the hellhole she was in, and they didn't want her to wake up around the accusing Kolbs.

Trent was convinced that they'd kill her thinking that she'd killed their friend Bubba.

"Okay, Trent. I'll be here when you get back. I got some ideas."

Eli pointed to the drunkards by the fire tending to Bubba, trying to understand what had happened.

Carrying the little girl away from the house, Trent followed the road until he got to her address, which was only a few houses away.

Starting to wake up, he sat her down on her front porch swing. He didn't ring the doorbell and allowed her to wake up completely on her own.

Trent saw that she had a small welt under her eye but there was nothing he could do about that. Leaving the teenagers house, he returned to the Kolb house. He ran all the way back and when he arrived, he saw that the police were already there asking Wyatt what happened to the man that they placed in the body bag.

"That girl must have bit his dick and balls off." Wyatt explained what he thought happened.

"What's the girl's name?" the cop asked.

"Brittany Jacobs," said Wyatt, unconcerned that she was a minor.

"The chief's daughter?"

Wyatt said, "Yes, that's her. She must have done it!"

"Bullshit!" the officer said, "That little girl only weighs ninety pounds. She couldn't have done it. This man's dick is ripped off and his balls were sliced off."

Wyatt countered the cop's argument. "I think she is on drugs."

"Drugs? Where did she get them, Kolb?" the officer asked, accusingly.

"How the fuck do I know? Are you trying to say I gave them to her?"

The inexperienced police officer knew that he had little to no evidence to accuse any of the Kolbs and warned, "If I find out that you did this, I'll be back without my badge on. She's my goddaughter, you son of a bitch!"

"Listen, take the body and get off my property. You've been here long enough. You've interviewed everyone. We're about to have dinner and you're not invited," Wyatt demanded.

Three hours later, the last police cruiser left as Trent and Eli hid in the nearby woods. Eli asked if the little girl was okay and Trent told him what he did and noticed that Eli sported a big smile on his face, and he wondered what he'd done in his absence.

"Why are you acting weird, Eli?"

"You'll soon see, I reckon!"

Continuing with their party, the group around eating fried chicken and jambalaya, and of course, drinking an abundance of beer. Wyatt and everyone talked about Bubba and some even snickered when they talked about how he died.

"Wyatt, what's in this stew?" asked one of his friends.

Wyatt answered, "Chicken, barbeque pork, and deer sausage, why?"

"What the fuck is this?" Morgan pulled a hunk of half-chewed meat out of his mouth and threw it to Wyatt.

He caught it and placed it on an empty plate.

He took a bite of the stew and tasted something strange as well. He spat it out on the same plate and it appeared to have the same texture and look as the mystery meat that Morgan had.

"Oh shit! This is Bubba's dick and balls!" Wyatt yelled and took a few steps back from the plate.

Morgan immediately vomited and Wyatt did as well. They looked at it closer and it was indeed the remnants of Bubba's manhood.

"Who the fuck put that in there?" Wyatt asked, as the girls screamed and threw their plates down and spit out what they chewed.

Trent, listening to the group agonizing that they had just eaten a stew with the essence of Bubba included, looked at Eli, smiled, and said, "Nice touch, Eli! I wish I'd thought of that."

Gathering his things, he hid them in the woods near the Kolbs house for future use, and remarked, "I think we've done enough for tonight. They have parties every weekend but we'll continue tomorrow."

"Okay, I had fun. Can't wait until tomorrow. What are you doing with that rifle?" asked Eli.

"I'm loading it because when we leave, I want to leave them our calling card. See that nice looking car over there?" Trent pointed at the very valuable Corvette.

Eli looked at it and said, "Sure."

"It looks like Ethan had it fixed from the last time I visited here. It's not going to be pretty for very long."

They gathered what they were going to take with them and slowly walked away, avoiding the group's view. As soon as they were clear of the compound, Trent opened fire on the Corvette, demolishing it with over a hundred bullet holes in just over a minute. He saw that the group got down on the ground and grabbed their weapons when they heard the rapid fire of a fully automatic AR-15. Trent emptied his magazines as he and Eli departed.

Wyatt, Morgan, and everyone else investigated where the gunfire came from and when they saw the car, they knew that someone targeted them.

"Look what they did to Ethan's car! It's totaled!" Morgan wildly fired into the woods, not caring where the bullets went.

"Did you see who they were, Morgan?" asked Everett.

"No, but if they come back, I'm going to shove this rifle up their ass and empty this magazine in it!"

***

Returning to their camp, Trent felt concern that he'd killed Bubba without feeling remorse, because he was the first man that Trent even had thoughts of killing, but Eli quickly reassured him that killing him prevented Bubba from killing the little girl.

Chapter 11
Terrorizing the Terrorists

"You've done this town and area a great service. You saw what he did. He had the will, and desire, to rape her. We saved that little girl's life. I know that he died a gruesome death that many will deem barbaric, but that is what people like Bubba deserve."

"I guess you're right," Trent agreed.

"That asshole deserved what he got. I only wish he would have died slower so I could have inflicted more pain on him," Eli stated, without regard to the viciousness of the injury.

"I know you're right. My father taught me the opposite, but even he had little regard for child molesters. I bet he would've done the same thing. Something strange happened back there. The knife drifted out of my hand and into Bubba's, and I wanted him to do what he did and he did it, and afterward, the knife came back to me like magic." He pulled out his knife and wiped the blood off it.

"It worked out, Trent. Just be glad it went perfectly. I must admit, I got a lot of pleasure watching that asshole squirm and scream. We probably saved many young girls' lives tonight."

Eli told him that there would be other deaths as well by the time they eradicated the evil to the salvation of the town. After the talk, Trent wanted to continue with the attacks, regardless of the viciousness. Eli's resolve made Trent understand that the evil in man was not just his actions, but also the inactions of those who could prevent it and didn't.

Having a way about him that Trent didn't completely understand, Eli always put things in perspective, and regardless of what he felt as he killed Bubba, Trent felt as though he'd ridden the world of a man devoid of soul and hell-bent on taking people's lives to embolden his own self-absorbed ego.

Trent often wondered whether he could've stopped the Kolbs well before Ethan killed Amanda because, had he known Ethan's intent, he would've killed him years earlier.

Trent rationalized the killing, thanks to Eli's words of encouragement, because Bubba didn't appear to care, and he felt that by taking care of Bubba before he had a chance to kill innocents, Trent most assuredly saved another grieving family from seeing their child die well before her time.

The fact that each of the Kolbs had killed before, further justified his actions. They always had an alibi and millions of dollars at their disposal to pay off officials to make the suspicion go away.

Trent and Eli didn't care about money. Trent often wondered why Eli seemed so happy to help him see to it that the Kolb brothers paid the ultimate price for their treachery. Eli relayed a story from his past, where Ethan Kolb killed his grandfather just because the old man ran him off his property at gunpoint.

"Randolph Kolb covered it up and made it seem as if my grandfather killed himself. He used his knowledge of law to take my grandfather's land. The land that we are on used to be his, and that's why I'm here helping you rid the state of this scourge," Eli explained.

"This is your grandfather's land?" Trent asked.

"It used to be before Randolph Kolb took it from him. Kolb owns just about all the land around the town. That's how they got it. Ever wonder why there have been so many unexplained deaths around here in the last ten years?"

Trent looked at Eli and asked, "You saying that Randolph Kolb killed all those people just to get their land?"

"Yes, I'm certain of it, because he craved power, and whoever has the most land has the power over its people. It's the kingdom syndrome. The king needs to own all the land and then he can rule the people on it. Should the people refuse to sell it, Kolb took it by any means possible. The brothers are just the spawn of the snake. We also have to go after the snake."

"Randolph Kolb?" Trent asked.

"Yes. He's the real terrorist. But, should he die, his sons will take his place, so we have to take them all out and allow the people to take back what is legally and morally theirs. The father is protected but we'll pry him away from his sanctuary in that mansion on the hill, when we destroy his seeds," Eli further stated.

"I've met Randolph Kolb and he doesn't seem like he cares for his sons. He told me that I'm his heir because he used to be my father's best friend. I will assess Randolph Kolb after we've done away with his sons."

"That sounds fair, but I must stress that Randolph Kolb has to be part of the equation."

"Perhaps so, but for now, let's get started on his sons. We have to be smart about this so the law doesn't come after us."

Laughing wildly at his concern, Eli confused Trent. He stopped laughing as he saw that murder was not a funny subject to Trent, but he still had the images of his dead wife in his mind, which made the idea more palatable.

"Well, let's get started. Wow, we've talked for five hours and I'm not tired in the least," Trent said, reloading his guns.

"Well, if you're not tired, let's go to town. It's been decades since I've set foot in town. I bet there's at least one Kolb there causing a problem or two," suggested Eli.

"I can almost guarantee it. Let's go. No deaths in town though, okay?" Trent asked.

"Okay, I understand."

Trent and Eli walked to town and no one acknowledged the two mountain men strutting along the road.

They saw that the Kolbs had taken over his Sportsmen store, so they decided to go there rather than the main street of town. The Sportsmen store was located on the outskirts of town, so the town's citizens wouldn't notice them.

They peered into the window and saw Everett and Kerry behind the counter and Morgan asleep on the bench just inside the door.

"This is a perfect opportunity. All of them are here. We need to go to their house now!" Trent said excitedly.

"What about Wyatt? I don't see him here."

"Knowing him, he's still probably in the residence behind the store, looking for my father's secret hiding place."

Ready to leave, Wyatt showed up pointing a rifle at both of them.

"What the fuck are you two old farts looking at?" he asked as his rifle menaced Trent.

Eli turned around and stared at Wyatt.

His stare stilled Wyatt; wide-eyed, he dropped his rifle. "You can't be here, you're dead!"

"Is that what you think? How do you know that?" Eli asked, as Wyatt ran inside, scared of something that escaped Trent.

"What was that all about?" asked Trent.

"He thought that he saw something that he didn't understand. Forget that ignorant asshole. Let's get to their house. I'm curious about what you've got planned," Eli resolved.

Agreeing, they ran to the Kolb brothers' empty house with Eli's mule-led cart rolled behind them. However, before they went the last few hundred feet, they came across a nest of poisonous copperhead snakes. Carefully, Trent harvested the dangerous snakes into a bag, and they continued their journey.

"What are they for?" asked Eli.

"You'll see," Trent said, as he twisted the bag to prevent their escape.

Continuing their trek toward the house, Trent found the supplies that he'd stashed in the woods near the house during their previous attack, and they approached the front door.

Trent turned the doorknob, but the Kolbs had locked it, so he easily kicked it in. First, he went to Kerry's room and found three rifles, a shotgun, and two pistols.

Emptying the guns of their ammunition, he replaced them with blanks that he'd taken from his store. Trent's actions confused Eli but he allowed him to continue without interruption.

He also placed four of the ten snakes that he'd captured in the woods, around the room.

Next, they visited Wyatt's room and did the same. However, when Trent entered Everett's room he saw a naked girl tied to the bed with a scarf duct-taped in her mouth. It was another very young girl who attended the party the night before. They saw that she had severe injuries to both of her wrists. Her hands had turned blue due to the tightness of her bindings. She was unconscious. They searched for identification but found none. Eli untied her as Trent let a few more snakes loose and replaced the bullets in his guns just as he had done in Kerry's and Wyatt's rooms.

"How is she?" Trent asked.

"Don't know, but since we don't know who she is, we'd better drop her off at the doctor's office. She's got a fever and those wounds don't look so good. What animals these idiots are. Are you almost done?" Eli asked, as he gathered the young girl into his strong arms.

"Take her out of here. I just have Morgan's room to fix. I'll be out soon," Trent said, as he helped Eli dress the little girl and placed a blanket around her.

"There's a special place in hell for anyone who'd do this to this sweet little girl."

Eli left the garbage-littered room.

Entering Morgan's room, Trent was amazed that a grown man could live among such filth. Reaching into his bag, Trent pulled out six poison ivy bushes, and placed them under Morgan's sweat-stained sheets.

He had two snakes left but one of them nipped Trent as he released them. He felt no pain and it didn't bleed, so he didn't think anything of it. He replaced the blank ammunition in all of Morgan's guns, then removed the four boxes of cartridges and replaced them with the blanks.

He left the room and met Eli in the woods on the other end of the property. The little girl was still unconscious, but amazingly, the color had returned to her hands, and her fever appeared to be breaking.

"We need to get her to the doctor's office before she wakes up. These people think I'm dead, and I want to keep it that way."

Trent sat down and felt the girl's forehead.

"We have to wait until dark, Trent. We can't just carry the girl to the town in broad daylight," he reasoned.

"You're right. Is there anything we can do to keep her sleeping until then?"

"Yes, let me take care of that. A doctor needs to tend to her wounds. There are some plants I know of that can help with those cuts. I discovered one thing, though."

"What's that?" asked Trent.

"The ropes didn't cut her arms. He tortured her."

"Everett did that? I used to be friends with him. I can't believe that he'd sank that low. How can a guy change that much in just a few years? I noticed something. These brothers are aging fast; Wyatt is nearly totally gray now and Everett is just starting to get gray hair."

Trent was a large man so he carried the girl back to their camp and Eli carried everything else.

Eli asked, "Why the blanks?"

"Because I want to have a face-to-face with all of them tonight and I want to make sure that they are shooting blanks at me. I intend to allow them to shoot me as often as they want," Trent stated, as they walked.

Scratching his head, Eli wondered why Trent was so concerned about the Kolb brothers shooting him when it suddenly hit him. He knew something that Trent obviously didn't know, but he kept the realization to himself until he could sit down and explain it to him in a less stressful situation. He decided to allow Trent to conduct his war, his way.

An hour later, they arrived back to their camp, and Trent gently laid the girl down on the soft ground and wrapped her up in the blanket.

Eli made a fire, collected water for the girl, and wiped beads of sweat from her forehead with cool water to assist in getting her fever down.

A few hours later, dusk descended on the campsite and Trent and Eli prepared to visit the Kolbs again.

The skies turned dark, as they carried the young girl to the doctor's office using Eli's mule cart.

By the time they got to town, most of the town's citizens were in their homes or at the bar. The few streetlights came on at eight o'clock, which gave them plenty of time to drop the girl off at the doctor's office unobserved.

As they traveled, they noted that there was very little traffic, so they used the paved road and were able to get to the town quickly with no one seeing them.

Chapter 12
Morgan's Torture

Trent quietly laid the girl down on the chaise lounge chair on the doctor's front porch as Eli led his mule and the cart away from the house. When the cart was clear from view, Trent rang the doorbell and hid beyond the property line.

Opening the door, the doctor saw the young injured girl, and immediately called for his wife to assist him in bringing her in the house. Trent quickly left the doctor's house and caught up with Eli, and they made their way back to camp. Upon arriving, they noticed that someone destroyed their camp.

"I think the Kolbs have found our hideout," Eli asserted.

"Yes, it appears so, but they didn't find the cartridges we took from them," Trent happily reported.

Just as they were about to set out, a shot rang out and then another and another. In the bushes, Morgan and Kerry Kolb shot at them.

Trent ducked behind a tree trunk.

"What the hell? Eli, run for cover. I think that they are firing at us!"

"I know they're firing at us."

The shots stopped and Trent spoke to a calm Eli as he collected his mule, "Do you suppose that the shots were from the Kolb's?"

"I certainly do."

***

From behind some bushes, Morgan stated, "I had them square and I missed. My sights must be way off."

"Mine too. I had the older one in the head and I missed. Let's get the fuck out of here! This is strange. I've never missed at that range," Kerry said, as they backed off and ran to their home.

"I know that they are the ones who killed Bubba, I just know it. Let's go tell Wyatt and Everett. We'll be ready for them if they come visit us again," Morgan said, as he ran.

***

Back at the campground, Trent and Eli sifted through the strewn mess to find anything salvageable. Trent kept an eye on the bushes for any kind of movement or sounds. Trent's tension didn't escape Eli's notice.

"It's okay, Trent. They've left." Eli casually released his mule from the harness and tied him up.

Concerned, Trent asked, “Yes, but how do you know it’s the Kolbs? I know they have friends and we didn’t replace their friends’ cartridges. Those were real bullets ricocheting off trees.”

“Trent, you worry too much. It’s obvious that they’re gone. Now, let’s go pay them a visit. What are you doing?” Eli asked.

“I got nipped by one of the copperheads but I don’t see a mark.”

Eli snickered and said, “Let’s go, no snake’s going to hurt you with those hides on.”

They set out for the Kolbs house and decided to walk right down the center of the dirt driveway.

The Kolb brothers waited for them and shot multiple times, but Trent and Eli confidently continued walking knowing that the Kolbs fired blanks.

Morgan looked at Kerry and said, “There’s no way we missed them. They must be ghosts or something.”

“Bullshit,” said Kerry, as he raised his shotgun and blasted both barrels at Trent’s chest.

Trent raised his rifle and shot at the upstairs window because that is where he saw the shots come from. He blasted out the window, then stood there in the middle of the driveway as Morgan and Kerry returned fire, yet none of their shots found their mark.

Turning around, Trent and Eli simply dissolved into the woods.

"They have no idea what's going on, Eli. What do you want to do now?" he asked, smiling because it appeared to him that the Kolbs hadn't realized they were shooting blanks.

"Nothing. Let them sleep on this for a few days. Besides, we left presents for them in their rooms and I think that we should allow those presents to do some of the work," Eli suggested.

At the Kolb house, the gunshots woke up the remaining sleeping brothers. Wyatt rolled over and saw a snake on his bed seeking warmth.

He fired off three shots in the snake's direction but none found their mark. Morgan, Kerry, and Everett ran into the room and a shirtless Morgan asked excitedly, "What the fuck are you shooting at?"

Wyatt jumped up from his bed with his smoking pistol pointing into the dark corner. "It's a snake. It's a goddamn snake in my bed! I missed it, I think."

Morgan walked over to the corner and removed the blanket that Wyatt flung from the bed, and there it sat, coiled up and ready to strike.

"Give me your machete, Wyatt. I'll take care of this." Wyatt threw the machete to Morgan and with one blow, he decapitated the snake.

"What's with your back, Morgan?" Wyatt asked as he walked over to the snake.

"What are you talking about? There's nothing wrong with my back," he said, as he scratched what he could reach.

"It's blistered all over it. You don't feel that?" said Wyatt as he picked up the snake and threw it out the window.

"That's a fucking copperhead," Morgan asserted.

Finding many of the deadly snakes, they went through each room and killed them all. They decided to sleep outside because they found so many of them that they weren't sure if they missed some.

"I ain't staying in there. The house is infested with them." Wyatt stormed out of the house.

Morgan, now knowing that blisters scorched his back, scratched what he could reach, feverishly. Itching badly, he begged his brothers to scratch his back but they chose not to.

Everett, seeing that his captive girl was missing, asked, "You guys see Emily around anywhere?"

"I guess you didn't tie the bitch up tight enough," scolded Kerry.

"The ropes were plenty tight enough; besides she is so drugged up she couldn't have gone anywhere. Either she's hiding here somewhere or someone came in here and took her," he suggested, as he searched the closet.

Wyatt said, "I think Kerry's right. Those snakes didn't get in here by themselves. Guys, we're being attacked. Someone shot Ethan's car full of holes, and with what happened to Bubba, I get a feeling that we're next."

Kerry stated, "Those two guys in the woods, I think I've seen them before. I shot each of them I don't know how many times. I know I couldn't have missed them that badly."

Rolling around on the ground trying to scratch his back, Morgan complained, "Dammit, I can't stand this. If they did this to me, I'll kill their asses with my bare hands."

***

Back at camp, Eli and Trent made plans to move because the Kolbs knew where they were. Eli wanted to go west but Trent knew what lay west of them. For some reason, he could not go near where the Kolb's buried him alive.

Eli and he walked toward it, then Trent stopped and said, "I can't go any farther. Just across the tree line is where they buried me. I can't go there. Something inside me won't allow it. Let's stop and make camp here."

Eli said, "We're not that far from where we were. Come on. Let's go, there's nothing to be fearful of."

"I said no! I will go no farther! I can see the grave from here! I'm too close!" He screamed an irrational scream, stopped, sat down, and didn't budge another step.

Eli had no choice. He tied up his mule and started a fire after he cleared away the knee-high brush.

They sat by the fire, talked about the night's events, and smiled when they thought about the snakes and the poison ivy they'd placed in Morgan's bed.

Dawn approached, and Trent wanted to explore the woods away from the place they buried him, but Eli wanted to make plans for the night's terror at the Kolbs, so Trent set out on a hike alone, far away from their new camp.

Eli suspected that he just wanted to get as far away as he could from that grave.

For hours, Trent walked through the thicket and slashed a couple small saplings that marred his path. He came across a hidden cave adorned with many years' worth of vines concealing its entrance. It appeared to him to be ruins of some sort, but once he cleared the vines, he saw that it was just an old, naturally formed cave.

Walking slowly into the dark cave, he tripped over some rocks, and found an old cobwebbed laden torch in a holder on the wall as he braced himself against the moist cave wall. He revised his previous thinking about the cave's origin because he saw pickax marks and realized that the cave was an old mining operation, complete with a coal car and rails running through the center of it.

The torch was old and once lit didn't supply very much light, but he felt enthused about exploring the cave further, regardless of the dimmed torch.

Deeper and deeper he descended into the cave and noticed antique lanterns, shovels, and ax heads with the handles worn off due to age and rot. He was happy to see the old lanterns, and luckily, some still had oil in them. He lit a few of them to provide more light.

He came across something he didn't expect to see. A full skeleton with the skull set in an old miner's helmet leaned against a darkened wall.

"Who are you?" he asked himself as he removed the skeleton's helmet, and read that its owner was a foreman named Daniel. The farther he went into the cave, the more he learned.

He spied a few more skeletons and a few coal cars full of coal. Looking up, he saw what cleaned the dead man's flesh off their bones so completely. Thousands of bats hung above his head, and he stood ankle deep in guano. The bats congregated in one room, so he moved on slowly and quietly to not rouse their attention.

In the next room, he found something odd that made him wonder, but also answered a question that his father never could: the skeleton of a young adult with his clothes still on, and a West Virginia University Mountaineers baseball cap on.

Why would this young man be all the way in here? he pondered. He's definitely not a miner. He sat the lantern down beside the bones of the young man.

Noticing scribbling on a rock above the skeleton, he wiped off years of dust and dirt with his hand to make it more readable.

It read: *I'm lost and can't get out. I'm scared! The bats chase me and bite me. I'm Elijah O'Flaherty. I'm twenty-four years old and I can't fight them anymore. My injuries are too severe for me to walk. I guess I'll die here. My friends call me Patch although they haven't called me that in years. I leave behind my wife and my five children. I sold my soul for a prophecy once before to make my return, but I needed to sacrifice five, most dear, for my salvation. I must return to that prophecy and return once again to prevent this fate.*

"Patch? This couldn't be my father's friend named Patch! And what did he mean about returning and prophecies?" he whispered, as he wiped more and saw a date. It read 1993.

This is impossible! My father saved you. He told m*e*, he stated to himself, but then a more serious question crept into his mind. This man has the same name as Eli. What the hell does this mean?

Feeling anxious to get back to Eli to question him about it, he ran through the bat room. Awakened, a few of the bats chased him through the cave until they got to the entrance, saw the bright sunshine, and ceased their pursuit.

On his way back, he had a sickening feeling that something bigger was happening that he didn't quite understand.

He decided not to tell Eli what he'd found, but question him about his favorite baseball team growing up.

Realizing that he knew very little about Eli, he thought it prudent to keep what he knew to himself because the old man always gave him vague answers when he questioned him.

Arriving back to camp, he met Eli.

Eli asked, "Did you have a nice walk?"

"Oh yeah, I loved it. It's funny, as far as I walked, I'm not the least bit tired and didn't sweat a drop even in the bright sun."

"Why is that so strange? The hides are blocking the sun well and that hat keeps the sun from your head."

Trent heard people talking over by the grave, so they put out the fire and crept closer looking through the high grass, completely hidden. It was Morgan with the sheriff's department and a few laborers.

"This ought to be fun to watch," he whispered. "It looks as though Morgan confessed to kidnapping me."

The laborers started digging. The police officers and onlookers obscured Trent's view of the grave. One of the laborers said, "There's a box here. Oh shit, there's a body in it!"

"What? A body? That's impossible!" Trent whispered and inched closer.

Chapter 13
Found Dead

They pulled a body out of the grave, and as the people who stood around the grave parted, he saw that it was his body they pulled out of the grave.

"What the fuck?" he screamed. Eli covered his mouth, not wanting to give away their hiding place.

The police handcuffed Morgan, still itching and begging people to scratch his back, and read him his rights as Trent saw them place his body into a black body bag.

The sheriff said, "Yep, that's Trent Pritchard all right. Morgan, I knew that you were a thug but I didn't think you could do something like this."

Morgan, still scratching, replied, "I didn't do this. I walked through here and saw the two PVC pipes sticking out. I hated that motherfucker because he killed my brother, but I didn't bury him there. Can someone scratch my back, please?"

"Sheriff," an officer interrupted, "I thought I heard something on the other side of that tree line. I'm going to investigate." The sergeant agreed, and the officer walked directly toward Trent and Eli.

Trent suddenly shook badly. Not because a cop walked directly toward him, but because he saw something that he couldn't explain and realized that he was there with Eli but also believed what his eyes saw. The cop was right on top of them but he didn't see the camp, the cart, the mule, or the men.

The sheriff called out, "Do you see anything?"

The officer turned around, walked back, and said, "There's nothing there, sir."

Speechless and scared, Trent sat among the tangled underbrush, and thought back to when he courageously escaped from the dirt and mire of his cramped prison.

Vividly remembering his fight to survive, he once felt pride that he'd persevered until he found an avenue of escape but now, nothing made sense. Perhaps he and the cops were wrong, he wondered.

Struggling to justify what his own eyes saw, he turned to Eli only to see him walking away. Confused at what he saw, he noticed that Eli seemingly didn't want to offer an opinion.

Trent walked over to Eli with hopes that he could ease his confusion, but Eli just veered the conversation back to their terrorization of the Kolb brothers.

Pleading with him to hear his concerns, Eli wouldn't answer any of Trent's rapid-fire questions. It was up to Trent to find a viable answer to what he saw. He knew that he'd escaped from the grave because he was upright, walking, talking, and breathing—or so he thought. He grabbed his arm and felt the heat of life and the flesh of a living human being. There were things that he didn't understand prior to seeing what he saw.

He always felt great and seemed to have boundless energy, which was something he'd always had, but not to that degree. He wanted to test his endurance, much to the dismay of Eli. He ran, full out, to the old cave he'd discovered a mile away and immediately returned at full speed.

He noticed not a drop of perspiration, an aching muscle, or a scratch from the many thorns he'd run through. He sat down as fear of his new abilities coursed through his thoughts. Eli, seeing that Trent was perplexed at what he saw, confessed.

"Trent, I don't know how to put this gently, so pardon my bluntness. You died in that grave. Your body didn't escape but your spirit did," Eli confessed.

"Bullshit, Eli! Look at me, I'm alive. I'm talking to you. I see you. Can a spirit pull up this plant?" he asked, as he yanked up a small tree and threw it aside.

"That plant doesn't exist in the living world, Trent. It's simply there because you wanted it to be there. You're dead, my friend, and I might as well tell you, I'm dead as well," Eli definitively stated, as Trent's eyes widened with wonder.

"What? You can't be dead, dammit! I'm not either, so just knock it off!" Trent spouted. He walked away, sorry that he'd brought it up.

"I can prove it very easily, Trent, if you'd let me."

"You can't possibly prove it to me. I know that I'm not dead!"

"Trent how long have you been here with me in the woods?"

"It would have to be six months, looking at my beard, but you said time doesn't matter."

"In this case, it probably does, besides, I want to hurry and continue our plan. Do you, in the six months that you've been here, ever remember eating or drinking or even sleeping for that matter?"

Trent thought about what Eli asked but he had no answer. It crushed him to believe what he thought, but Eli was right, he hadn't eaten or drank anything in the time he'd been in the woods. He pulled out a knife and sliced his arm. A gash formed but it immediately sealed up without a trace of blood.

"You believe me now? You can't harm yourself. Fate has given you a great gift. You've been given a chance to revenge the death of your wife, your parents, your child, and even yourself," Eli reasoned.

Trying to further justify his existence, Trent spouted, "But the Kolbs saw me! They shot at me!"

"Yes, they did. However, it's up to you whether or not you want anyone to see you. See, I can turn it all off, watch."

In an instant, Eli vanished before his eyes and reappeared just as quickly.

"You'll be able to do that, as well as many other gifts that you'll learn along the way. This is why time means nothing to me."

Finally, after many explosive realizations, Trent accepted his demise.

Hurt and dejected, Trent stated, "Okay, Eli, we'll continue. I guess we didn't have to put blanks in the guns, huh?"

"Trent, it will be okay. I went through the same thing when I died. I didn't have someone here to explain it all to me. I had to find out on my own. I told you that time means nothing now. Perhaps when this is all over, I'll tell you how to go back to the living world and check on your loved ones."

Trent, depressed and scared, stated, "Loved ones? I don't have any loved ones anymore. They all died!"

"You have me, son." Eli gently put his hand on Trent's shoulder.

"Where is my Amanda? And my mother and father?"

"They have gone to a place that we can't get to yet. We can't go there because we have loose strings to tie up."

"What? What strings? What are you trying to say?" He stared angrily at Eli.

Eli said something that he shouldn't have said and tried to backtrack. He successfully changed the subject when he brought up Amanda and his unborn child.

Focused, he remembered what Eli said, but Trent didn't ask him to elaborate and allowed him to change the subject. He speculated that Eli was hiding something very important.

It was very obvious to Trent that Eli wanted the Kolb brothers dead more than he did. His revenge on the Kolbs took a backseat to why he was there in his afterlife without his family. However, he still wanted the Kolbs to pay for destroying his life and killing everyone he loved.

Trent was also curious about what else he could do if he was, in fact, a spirit, and asked, "Can we be invisible?"

"Yes, you can become invisible, but that won't be good for what we have to do to the Kolbs. Are you ready to go?" Eli asked.

Trent put on his backpack and grabbed his walking stick.

"Let's go! I want to get this over with to see where this all ends," Trent said, as he hurriedly passed Eli.

Following Trent, Eli said nothing all the way to the Kolb house.

Arriving to their destination, Trent asked Eli, "Why did you allow me to change all the cartridges if they could just shoot through us?"

"Simple, Trent. I didn't want you to know that you're dead because when you thought that you had a future, you were passionate about making them pay for what they did. Now that you know that you're dead, I didn't want your disgust for them to wane. Think about it. Without us, two little girls could have been the Kolb's next victims.

"So, we're doing something good by eradicating this scourge for the good of the town. It upsets me that you found out the way that you did."

"I agree with that. Is that why I felt the way I did when we approached the place where they buried me?" he asked.

"Yes; had you stepped over your grave, your spirit would've been sucked down to where you were, and then your body and soul would lay there intact and be delivered to the realm where your spirit would dwell forever. Because your spirit is not with your body, you can enact revenge on the people who put you in that grave. If you stayed with your body, the Kolbs would continue their torturous war on the town. Now that they have taken your body away, you have nothing to fear about being truly dead, unless of course, you happen to visit the morgue. If you ever step across your body, fate will suck you back in your body forever."

"Okay, let's go. Morgan's over there sleeping in the tent. I guess he's out on bail, and he's still freaked out about going into the house," said Eli.

Trent and Eli took off their backpacks and walked over to the tent. Trent removed his knife and sliced the tent down the center. Morgan awoke to see the knife slicing the tent, and then Trent opening it up.

Morgan, seeing Trent, urinated on himself and shook. He grabbed his pistol and fired through Trent's head.

Morgan seemed to think he missed, so Trent grabbed a small wooden table and placed it behind his head and said, "Shoot me again, you fat son of a bitch."

He fired two more shots. Trent showed him the table with two holes in it, indicating that the bullets had to have gone through him to impact the wood.

Screaming in terror, Morgan pleaded, "I'm sorry! I'm sorry! I don't know why I buried you in the woods! Please don't kill me!"

"You killed me, asshole. You won't live through this night!" Trent allowed Morgan to run into his house.

Appearing instantly, Trent waited for him at the top of the dark stairs.

Looking up to see Trent standing at the top, he fearfully begged, "No, don't do this, Trent! I beg you!"

Trent slowly walked down the stairs toward Morgan.

"Are you under the assumption that your death will be instantaneous? You Kolbs killed my parents, my wife, and my child. Each of you will suffer four wounds before I kill you. One for each of my family members. This is your first!" Trent pulled out his knife, stabbed Morgan in both eyes, and said, "That's for my child who never got a chance to see."

Morgan screamed as he placed his hands over his eyes. Blood streamed down his chest as the lights came on in the hallway, and the three other brothers ran down the stairs to find out why he screamed. Finding Morgan on the floor with a steady stream of blood pooling on the floor, they stood him up and made him remove his hands. His eyeballs were missing.

Placing a dirty towel over his face, Kerry looked at Morgan's clenched fists, and imagined how much pain he suffered.

Wyatt grabbed his hands and opened them. Morgan's eyeballs bounced to the floor with a thud and stuck to the hard wood floor. Morgan stepped back and squashed them as Wyatt tried to retrieve them to possibly have them reinserted.

"Shit, Morgan, you stepped on them! They're gone now," said Wyatt.

"Pritchard did this! He's here somewhere!" Morgan screamed.

"It couldn't have been Pritchard, we buried his ass. He's out there in the fucking woods," Wyatt said.

Morgan held the towel on his face. "No he's not. I told the cops where we buried him."

"You did what? Why the fuck did you do that?" Wyatt asked, angrily.

Morgan, still in agony, replied, "I don't know. I heard a voice in my head telling me to do it. Pritchard is after all of us. He's a ghost. He's a fucking ghost!"

Shaking badly, Morgan knew that Trent haunted him and realized that he'd never see again.

Kerry said, "Wyatt, we have to get him to the hospital. He's bleeding everywhere."

Wyatt smacked Morgan in the head and angrily stated, "He's lucky I don't put a fucking bullet in his dumb head after he told the cops where we buried Pritchard."

Morgan responded through tears, "I had to, dammit. I told you, a voice told me to. I told the cops that I walked through the woods and saw the two PVC pipes sticking out of the ground. They took me downtown but they bought it, so it's not coming back here. I need to go to the hospital. Pick up my eyes off the floor."

"They won't be putting those back in your ugly head. They're a stain on the floor after your fat ass stepped on them," Wyatt said, still angry at what his brother did.

The group of brothers drove him to Lost River because that was the nearest hospital. The bleeding nearly stopped by the time they arrived. The doctors operated on him to stop the blood loss but his eyesight was lost forever.

Trent, satisfied that he had inflicted enough pain for one night, left with Eli, who was strangely irritated with Trent that he didn't kill Morgan.

He asked, "You had a chance to kill that bastard. Why didn't you?"

As he walked away, he responded, "Because I'm not done with him, that's why. If you're so worried about it, why didn't you kill him?"

Eli, without thinking, replied, "I can't kill him, that's why!"

Trent stopped walking, looked at Eli, and asked, "Why can't you kill him? You had no problem killing Bubba!"

"I didn't kill Bubba, you did. I cut him up after you killed him," Eli reminded him.

"No, he was still alive when you cut it off!"

"He bled out when you castrated him. He died soon after. Morgan wasn't near death and you allowed him to live."

Trent smiled and said, "That's just temporary. He will die after he suffers as much as I did. I'm a fucking ghost and I don't care anymore. The Kolbs will not die before they endure more pain than they inflicted on Amanda and my parents, and since you can't kill them for reasons you're keeping from me, you'll just have to wait until I feel that they have suffered enough."

Becoming more and more distrustful of Eli, Trent was convinced that Eli wasn't telling him the whole story about his past.

Trent walked through the brush and Eli followed. He walked a different path because he wanted to gauge Eli's reaction. The path took them past the hidden cave that he'd discovered earlier.

"Where are we going?" asked Eli, as they plodded along.

"I just wanted to use a different path, that's all," he said, as he looked back to see any angst in Eli's demeanor. He saw nothing odd as they walked past the old cave where he thought Eli's body dwelled.

They continued back to the camp but something had changed. Trent had moved the camp a few hundred feet closer to the cave and away from his grave. Eli saw that the camp was in a different location but thought nothing of it.

Trent wanted to know more about the spirit world, but Eli didn't appear to want to inform him further. He was, however, interested in getting back to maiming the Kolb brothers. Eli appeared angry that Trent wanted to kill them systematically, which took more time than he cared to use.

"What are you worried about, Eli? You told me many times that time doesn't matter here. Morgan will heal and we'll return. He told me something before I took his eyes. He said that a voice made him and the others kidnap me. It wasn't about the money my father had stashed. It's something else that he couldn't explain."

"Who knows what that idiot thought?" stated Eli, as he walked over to his mule.

"Is Story, the mule, a spirit as well?" Trent asked, as he approached.

"Yes, he never tires and has always been a faithful friend in the darkness of the forest nights. He strolled into my camp lame and starving. I killed him and captured his spirit and he's been with me ever since."

Trent petted Story and asked, "Why do we walk instead of just appearing where we want to appear?"

"We walk because we can. Why should we just appear and miss what we see on our journey? There's so much to see. I think that I've seen every inch of nearly five square miles of forest. Sure, we could do as you ask, but we saw so little of all this beauty when we were alive, why should we continue to not see it while we're dead?" he explained.

Trent saw that Eli always waxed poetic when he talked about nature and wildlife, and seldom complained about his surroundings. Trent felt that he was right, though, as he thought back to his many hunting trips, only interested in collecting his prey and leaving the woods without noticing the budding trees and the telltale signs of the onset of spring.

Reminiscing that Amanda enjoyed nature's newness every year, he'd stopped hunting and accepted the way she looked at things. He never missed hunting and rather enjoyed his surroundings, as long as he saw his bright-eyed Amanda running through the wildflowers as if they grew just for her enjoyment.

He cried when he thought about all the times they could have had among nature, cut short by a drunken Ethan Kolb who sadly took it from him. The thought incensed him all over again as he planned his next adventure to the Kolb house. Eli wanted to go the next day, but Trent still wanted the systematic elimination of the Kolbs and to concentrate solely on Morgan for now.

Determining who'd kidnapped him, he'd targeted him to leave the world of the living first. Morgan was in the hospital, so he had to wait until he healed before visiting the house again. Until that time occurred, he and Eli took their walks, and Trent always ended up near the hidden cave but Eli still had no reaction to the place that housed his mortal remains. Trent figured that enough time had passed that he had just simply forgotten where his body lay.

Chapter 14
Morgan Returns

Two weeks later, Morgan returned to the house from the hospital. Blind and vulnerable to pranks by his brothers, he laughed off all their jokes about what happened to him because he needed his brothers to protect him should Trent return.

Walking into the house, he took stock of his surroundings. He had lost a lot of weight during his stay in the hospital and wanted it to stay that way.

Kerry was the main jokester; he applied makeup to him while he slept the first night. The next night they planned a weekend beer party to celebrate Morgan's return. They invited the usual girls and friends; however, fewer girls showed up because word got around town that it wasn't safe to be around the Kolbs when they drank.

Kerry noticed that the ones who did attend fawned all over the blind Morgan to make him feel better about his lack of sight.

"Shit, he's getting more action blind than as a fat guy who could see."

Wyatt saw the girls all over Morgan, asking him what it was like being blind.

Though Morgan was in a weakened state due to the loss of one of his senses, the more he drank, the meaner he got. He caught and beat Kerry when one of the girls let on that he had makeup on his face.

Kerry, lying drunk and dazed in the dirt, shook the cobwebs out, walked over to Morgan, and blasted a right to his jaw. Morgan and Kerry went at it to the delight of the brothers. Morgan was still a big man and made short work of the smaller Kerry.

"Okay, get the fuck off me, Morgan! I give up!" said Kerry, as Morgan pummeled him. "Damn, the fucker is still strong as an ox." Kerry pushed Morgan off him.

Morgan stopped and they drank another beer while the girls fawned over both of them. Kerry flicked the girls away as they tended to his wounds.

"I don't need any help!" he bellowed, sipping his beer and knowing that he couldn't beat his brother even though Morgan was blind.

Very young and mesmerized by the older brothers, the girls endured the abuse that all the Kolbs dished out. The country music blared through the darkened woods.

Trent and Eli approached but allowed only Morgan to hear them. The others saw nothing and just danced and drank around him.

Morgan got up and started dancing with a few of the girls as they pulled him up from his seat and moved around to the music; then he heard Trent and stopped dancing and found his seat. He sat there, scared and timid and expecting another injury.

"Wyatt, Kerry, Everett, he's here! Pritchard is here!" he yelled, as he quivered in his chair.

Wyatt made sure he had his revolver on his hip and ran over to Morgan, as did all his brothers. The girls and the other guests were oblivious to the fears of the brothers and continued drinking, dancing, and conversing as normal.

"Where is he, Morgan?" Kerry asked.

"You dumbass! I'm blind! How the fuck do I know? I heard his voice in my head and it seemed as if he was right in front of my face," he said, as he pointed in front of himself.

"I am in front of your face, you asshole. You won't be dancing before this night is done," Trent said.

"Do it, Trent!" implored Eli; he also talked right in front of the people dancing around to the latest country music ballad.

"That voice! I know that voice. Wyatt, the voice is back. It's saying that they are going to do something to me! Help me!" Morgan took a defensive position.

Trent asked, "What voice do you hear, Morgan?"

Stepping in front of him, Eli punched Morgan solidly across the face. He rolled out of his seat and landed in the dirt.

"Which of you assholes hit me? I'll kill your ass!" Morgan bellowed, as he got up and swung his fists wildly in every direction.

Trent looked at Eli. "Why did you do that? I asked him a question!"

Eli, angry, said, "Let's just kill the asshole and be done with it!"

"No, we talked about this. We do it my way or I leave!" threatened Trent.

He thought that something was up because Eli always backed down when he threatened to leave and not harm the Kolbs further. Eli's insistence that he kill them quickly made Trent believe that Eli had an ulterior motive to wanting them killed fast.

Morgan, hearing the argument between Trent and Eli, said, "I don't give a shit what you do. Just leave me be."

Wyatt, hearing that Morgan appeared to be talking to no one, asked, "Who the hell are you talking to? There's no one in front of you!"

"Yes, they're here. Two of them. Pritchard and another voice that I recognize." Morgan stepped back, feeling his way toward his brothers.

"You honestly think that hiding behind your brothers is going to help you? They'll feel what you feel eventually. You kidnapped me and buried me alive. Why shouldn't I do the same thing to you?"

"Wyatt, make him stop!" Morgan pleaded.

"Stop what? Where is he?" asked Wyatt.

Just as he said that, Morgan swung his fists, connecting with the back of Wyatt's head. "I got a lick in on him. I hit him square," Morgan stated, triumphantly.

"You dumbass, you knocked Wyatt clean out." Kerry got down on his knees and tended to Wyatt.

"Shit! I did? I'm sorry, Wyatt! Are you okay?" Morgan felt his way toward his fallen brother.

Wyatt, groggy, asked," What the fuck happened?"

"Morgan nailed the back of your head." Kerry helped Wyatt to his feet.

"Why, the fuck, did you hit me?" asked Wyatt, pushing Morgan backward.

"I thought you were Pritchard. He's right in front of me. He told me that he's going to do something to my legs."

"There are two of them talking to me and one is familiar. He sounded like Dad," Morgan said, frantically moving his head to the right and the left.

"Dad? He isn't dead, dumbass!" Kerry stated.

"They said that they were going to kill us all but I'm first. They said that they are going to attack us four times before they kill us," Morgan, frantically offered.

Everett, as he took another drink from his beer, said, "This is all bullshit! Morgan has taken too many blows to his dumbass head. Leave him on that chair and let's get back to drinking. Those bitches over there are ripe for fucking and I'm not going to let Morgan spoil it."

Everett went over to where the girls danced and started dancing with them, secretly placing a drug in one of the prettier one's beer.

Morgan felt alone in his fight, but didn't know how alone he was. Trent gathered a five-pound sledgehammer and walked toward the unseeing Morgan. Wyatt, still dazed from Morgan's blow, saw the sledgehammer coming toward him with no one dragging it.

"What the fuck?" he asked, as he stood up and watched it go right past him toward Morgan who sat in a chair, scared for his life.

He sensed that something approached so he prepared himself for whatever it was.

Wyatt grabbed the handle of the sledgehammer but he wasn't strong enough to subdue it.

It rose up high with Wyatt still clinging on to the handle.

"Watch out, Morgan," he bellowed, as it came down with great force and landed on Morgan's left ankle and foot, splintering his bones.

Bone and flesh flew away from Morgan as he screamed in agony and wondered what happened to him. Wyatt wasn't strong enough to keep the hammer from raising again, and it duplicated the damage on Morgan's right ankle and foot as well. Morgan's screams overpowered the loud music and the rest of the group ran to where Morgan laid. All they saw was Wyatt holding the sledgehammer and Morgan on the ground with his feet flattened, gushing blood through his worn-out tennis shoes. They removed his shoes and saw that his ankles were nearly gone with parts of his feet remaining in the shoes.

Trent stated, triumphantly, "This is for Amanda because she loved to run through the fields. Now you will not be allowed to run, or walk for that matter."

"Kill him, Trent!" Eli yelled, as Trent looked at the damage he inflicted on Morgan.

"Nope, not yet. There's more pain he has to suffer first." Trent walked away from the carnage.

Kerry and Everett blamed Wyatt for destroying Morgan's feet because they didn't see Wyatt trying to stop the sledgehammer's destruction, but only saw him hanging on to the handle.

They saw Wyatt as the perpetrator of the deed, and they tackled him and beat him until he released the sledgehammer.

Wyatt and Morgan made the trip to Lost River hospital for an extended stay.

***

Trent waited until their full recovery to return. Eli, incensed that Trent didn't kill Morgan, continually badgered him that he was taking too long to kill the brothers.

"Why does it matter to you when it happens, Eli? You've told me many times that time doesn't matter here. We have all the time in the world," he uttered, as he walked back to camp. "Is there something you're not telling me? Morgan seemed to recognize your voice. Just how well did you know the Kolb's?"

"I've never met Morgan Kolb. I don't know why he said that I sounded like his father. I don't sound like Randolph Kolb."

"So you know his father well?"

"No, I don't! Now let's get back to camp!"

"You still haven't answered my question. Why do you want me to kill them quickly?" Trent stopped walking and looked at Eli.

"I have my own reasons. Right now, it won't do you any good to know, so stop asking me. We want the same things to happen. Maybe I'm just not that much for torture and that's what you're doing," Eli confessed.

"That's right, they've tortured my family and the townspeople ever since I've known them. Now they will feel what it's like."

"You used to be friends with Everett. Are you going to torture him as well?"

"How did you know that? I never told you Everett and I were friends! If you have something to tell me, then tell me. If you don't, shut the hell up and kill them yourself!" he angrily spouted, as he continued walking.

"I told you, I can't kill them. They have to die by someone else's hands other than mine. Let's just let it go. I'll abide by whatever you want."

He thought that, once again, he'd told Trent too much.

"It's stuff like that. Why can't you kill them? Why do you seem to need me to do it?"

"I have my reasons. Do you want my help or not?"

Trent, seeing that Eli was upset, apologized to him. "I'm sorry, Eli. I guess the thought that I have no future is getting to me. I loved being alive and thought that after I died, I'd be in a better place than these woods."

Feeling nostalgic for the town and its people, Trent wanted to visit. He remembered when he walked among the people and thought that they just didn't recognize him because of his appearance, but now realized that they didn't recognize him because they couldn't see him. They would still not be able to see him but he wanted to be among them.

Leaving Eli in the woods, he walked toward the town.

Walking into the tavern, he saw that the townspeople had already heard about the strange things happening at the Kolb house, but mostly they were thankful that the Kolb brothers stayed away from them.

Nancy, still behind the bar, enjoyed the increased business now that the Kolbs had issues of their own.

A lonely man sat at the end of the bar and Trent wondered why it appeared that he had no friends. He sat next to the man and realized that he was Randolph Kolb, the father of the Kolb brothers who'd visited him that dark night years earlier.

How is it that the richest man in town seemed so lonely? he wondered.

The man was old, his face weathered and wrinkled, and he seemed to have the weight of the world on his mind.

Chapter 15 Randolph's Existence

He was respectful to Nancy and she seemed genuinely concerned for the man as he quietly sipped his beer and ignored the jeers of a few of the patrons. Trent wished he had the ability to read his thoughts as he sipped the last of his beer, paid his tab, and left a hefty tip.

"Goodbye, Randolph," Nancy said as she wiped down the bar.

He tipped his hat as he left without saying another word. Another patron took his barstool and was curious as to who the strange man was.

"Who is that guy, Nancy?" he asked, as Nancy looked toward the door.

"He's Randolph Kolb, the richest man in town." She poured a beer from the tap and set it down in front of him.

"So that's the father of the rednecks." The man took the first sip of his beer.

Nancy set her bar rag down, and said, "He's not like his sons. He just seems so troubled now. I think he's just embarrassed at how his sons turned out. He lost control over them years ago and hasn't been the same since his wife died a few years back. He's always been a friendly sort to me and to most of the people in town, but there are some who see Morgan or Wyatt when they see Mr. Kolb."

Thinking about what Eli said about killing the snake by cutting off its head, the Kolb brother's father didn't exhibit the kind of behavior that his sons possessed.

Following the man to his car, Trent saw that a few people waved and a pained smile traced across Randolph's face, and he waved back. Randolph Kolb seemed to be a fine man and Trent vowed never to harm him directly. However, it appeared to Trent that Eli wanted him dead. The mysteries piled up with regard to Eli. He knew that something very important eluded him, but he was sure that eventually Eli would tell him what he wanted to hear.

He watched as Randolph Kolb got in his black Bentley Brooklands and drove off. Given that Trent was a spirit, he projected himself to the Kolb mansion before Randolph drove through the massive gates.

Kolb walked inside, turned on a movie, sat there alone, and watched it, slowly sipping on his brandy.

Randolph displayed little emotion in his huge prison.

Flipping through the channels, he settled on the movie, *On Moonlight Bay,* the Doris Day and Gordon MacRea classic. Trent sensed the old man wept, not because of the story, but because of the time in which the movie was set. Post-World War II America was his childhood, and he looked as if he yearned for those days again.

He received a phone call from the hospital in Lost River. It was Wyatt, and he demanded money.

Randolph said in an uncaring slow voice, "Okay, I'll send it."

Wyatt yelled loudly over the phone, "I need it now, old man!"

"Okay, I said that I'd send it. Now leave me alone." Kolb walked to his safe, removed $100,000, walked down his long driveway to the mailbox, and placed the stacks of cash in it.

Randolph agreed to give it to him without even asking why he needed it. Just as Kolb had told him while he was alive, Trent saw that the Kolb brothers also terrorized their father as well. Randolph returned to the phone and told Wyatt to pick up the money, hung up the phone, and then he sat in front of the massive television for the next five hours. Randolph received no phone calls, emails, or visitors the whole time Trent was there observing him.

Randolph Kolb simply seemed to be an empty vessel with money that his sons tapped daily. He was a man devoid of life and held no control over his sons, and his mind was devoid of emotion.

Depressed at the lifestyle of the multimillionaire, Trent thought it ran contrary to the vibrant life-of-the-party persona his father had relayed to him about Randolph in their youth. His father always had a story to tell about Randolph's kind nature and his inexhaustible energy.

Trent remembered that his father kept a safe within his Sportsmen's shop and Randolph knew exactly where it was.

Already in town, he decided to get it and take it back to the camp. He hadn't looked in the safe in twenty years and had no clue what was in it. The Kolbs had shut down the Sportsmen store because two of them were in the hospital, and Kerry and Everett were too lazy to open the store.

Walking in the front door, then back to the living section of the store, Trent opened up the living room floor to see a hidden space with a small black safe in it.

It was a heavy safe, but Trent had no problem bringing it up and opening it. He may have been a spirit but because of it, his strength knew no limits.

In it, he found $20,000 and a newspaper clipping of the day Patch saved his father's life and another clipping depicting him saving Patch a few years later, in 1983. Given that the articles displayed Patch's real name, he was convinced that Eli, the spirit in the woods, was the same man his father befriended in his childhood.

Depicted in the photos were Randolph Kolb, his father and mother, Eli, and the rest of his friends. They all appeared happy that Patch had saved his father.

Trent had never called Eli "Patch" before, the way his father had, and he suspected Randolph had as well, but he was ready to gauge Eli's reaction when he showed him the clippings.

He emptied the safe but found something odd in the space under the floor. Another newspaper clipping, stating that his father had died during the fishing mishap, confused him. Written on the same day as the other article, the newspaper clipping indicated that Ben died with no mention of Eli's heroics. It also mentioned that the authorities arrested old man Glover, who threw Ben in the pond, for his father's murder.

How is this possible? he thought, as he pulled the old, faded and brittle newspaper from its formerly hidden spot. There was something that just didn't seem right to him. How could two newspapers dated the same day have reported two completely different outcomes? he wondered.

He knew which one was right because his father had lived and the police hadn't charged Mr. Glover with murder.

The two newspapers were identical with the exception of the Pritchard story. Another mystery confounded him.

He thought, if, by some unworldly happenstance, the second story was correct and his father died, who placed the newspaper in the secret space?

Reading further, he realized that Patch, must have placed both newspaper articles there.

He reasoned that the one that reported his father's death must have been a kneejerk reaction to a missing child and the second was a retraction once they realized that his father had survived. It stood as the only reasonable explanation.

In fact, many things he collected in his mind made no sense, outside of and including his very existence. He emptied the safe and walked out of the store. He donated the money to the townspeople because he had no use for it, and reasoned that his father would've wanted it distributed to Red Dirt's suffering citizens. There were many letters that Ben had written to his wife, and a few that he'd written in the event of his death. One note told Trent what had happened to his mother prior to Ben marrying her.

A newspaper clipping and a sheriff's log accused young Eli O'Flaherty of beating up Margaret Smith because she didn't want to marry him, but some of the letters discounted reports that Eli beat her.

Others, close to Margie, believed that he'd done much worse to her; such things didn't get publicized back then, but there was no mention of rape in any of Margie's or his father's letters.

Reading as he walked the side roads heading back toward his encampment, he stopped a few times when he read the exploits of the "Lost River Boys," as their parents called them.

There was no mention of Eli's wife and children, nor did they say much about Randolph's life either. One clipping announced the marriage of Trent's father and mother that made him stop because it showed a picture of Randolph, Patch, and Ben.

Strange that they invited Patch even though the newspaper reported that he'd beat up Mom just a day earlier, he mused.

Then he saw the dates on the article. It was evident that his father and Randolph didn't find out about the beating until after Ben's wedding.

Apparently, his mother didn't want to ruin the weddings and held it regardless of Patch's heinous act. Reading the newspaper article incensed Trent and he planned on confronting Eli when he returned. He also wanted to move the camp closer to the hidden cave.

Folding the newspaper clippings, he entered the camp. Eli wasn't there, and neither were his mule and cart. Most of the camp was gone as well. Trent knew where he'd gone, though.

Walking along the path through the high grass to the Kolb house, he arrived an hour later and saw Eli sitting on one of their junk cars. "What are you doing here?" Trent asked.

"I'm waiting until one of them comes back to the house. I can't depend on you killing them so I have to make them kill each other." Eli stood up.

"You can make them kill each other? How can you do that?"

"We both can. How do you think I got Morgan to tell the authorities where your body was?"

"You did that? Did you also tell him and the others to kidnap me?" he asked, accusingly.

Eli thought about that question, trying to envision Trent's reaction, and confessed, "Yes, I did. I had to do it. I can't tell you why until all of the Kolb brothers are dead."

"Do you want the father killed as well?"

Eli replied, "Yes, he's responsible for his sons. He's exactly like them."

"No, he's not," answered Trent.

He continued to tell Eli what he'd done.

"I followed him today and watched his every move. He's not anything like them. In fact, people in town who know him, like him. He visited me about a year after Amanda passed and made me the heir to his fortune. He didn't have a mean bone in his body."

"Bullshit, he's the worst one of them all."

Trent asserted, "I'm not going to allow you to plant those thoughts in their mind. They don't deserve a quick death after what they did."

"You think you can stop me?" asked Eli.

"I sure can, Patch."

Eli's eyes widened. He asked Trent to repeat what he called him.

"I called you Patch because that's what my father and Randolph Kolb called you when you were kids."

"Yes, they used to be my friends. Your father stole Margaret from me." Eli held his head down low.

"Is that why you beat her up the day before her wedding?" Trent asked, getting agitated.

"I didn't mean to hit her. She just wouldn't listen to reason. I wanted to marry her but she declined and started dating Ben. It hurt me that she didn't accept my proposal."

Trent replied, "I have plans for these idiots and you're not going to stop me or alter how it's going to be done. I have been learning about my abilities. I will stop you and you know that I can. If you try to influence them, I won't kill them right away. It could take years."

"I can just make them kill each other!"

"Yes, but one will still be standing!" Trent reminded him.

"As it is, Morgan will be dead when he arrives back from the hospital, and then it will be Wyatt's turn. You are either with me or against me. Take your pick! By the way, why did you move our camp here?"

"I thought that it would be easier. I guess you're right. It's just that I've been in these woods for decades and I want to move on," stated Eli.

"What does moving on have to do with killing the Kolb brothers? I thought time meant nothing to you!"

"Never mind, Trent, we'll do things your way."

Once again, Eli said something that didn't make sense to Trent.

What does killing the Kolbs have to do with Eli leaving the woods? he wondered to himself.

Another mystery and another piece of the puzzle emerged. He asked Eli many times what he meant by that, but there were reasons that Eli wouldn't explain further and Trent had not a clue as to what those reasons were.

***

A month went by and the hospital released Morgan again. He'd had both feet amputated because they couldn't repair his mangled feet. Wyatt, released earlier, had convinced Everett and Kerry that he had nothing to do with maiming Morgan.

Chapter 16
Morgan's Demise

In a wheelchair, Morgan didn't want to return to the party house with Wyatt. He insisted that they take him to his father's mansion.

Trent got wind that they were taking him there, so he went first and awaited his arrival.

They drove up to the massive house. Waiting for them was their father with a shotgun aimed at the car.

Kerry got out and approached Randolph Kolb. "What are you doing, you old fucker? You going to shoot me?"

"What are you doing here, Kerry?"

"I'm here to drop off Morgan. He doesn't want to go back to the house," Kerry said, as he opened the passenger door.

"No, he can't stay here! None of you idiots can stay here. I have disowned you all," Randolph stat-ed, sternly.

"You're the spawn of the devil and none of you will not invade my house or I swear I will end your lives right here and right now!"

Kerry walked up to him and said, "Fuck you! He's staying here at the mansion. He's your son, goddammit!"

Randolph, old and not used to raising his voice, did. "He's not my son and neither are you! All of you would rather put a bullet in my back than associate with me! I say take him to hell, I'm sure he'll be welcomed there! Now, get the hell off my property!"

He shot a round at Kerry's feet, causing him to scurry out of the way.

"I've got one more shot. Not a jury in the world will convict me from ending you right here and now," Randolph threatened.

Stepping back, Kerry seldom saw his father in such a rage.

Randolph continued, "I made a promise to your mother on her deathbed that I will support all of you financially and I have, to the detriment of all that I hold dear. I've used lawyers to keep you from jail and I've sacrificed my sanity to keep you comfortable, but I will not allow you to invade my home!"

Kerry, seeing that he meant what he said, closed Morgan's door and ran to the driver's side, flipped Randolph off, got in the car, and sped away. Morgan also flipped him off and yelled out the window, "Fuck you!"

Randolph lowered his shotgun and whispered, "I had such high hopes for you all before the devil took your souls."

Walking back into his house with his head held low, he never watched the car drive away.

Trent wondered what kind of hell they put him through to make a man shun his sons in their time of need, but he sensed that it must have been brutal to be responsible for having them and allowing them to grow up the way they did.

Realizing that Eli was back at the house, Trent assumed that with Morgan arriving soon, he might have Wyatt, or one of the other brothers, kill him on sight.

Travel was easy for him now that he was aware of his abilities. He arrived before the car did and saw Eli waiting in the middle of the road as they drove up their driveway. Eli raised his hands into the air as the car drove right through him.

Morgan's mind saw Eli and yelled for Kerry not to hit him.

"You're blind, Morgan, how can you see if anyone's in the fucking road? I didn't see anyone!" Kerry said as he drove on.

"I'm sensing that they are here. Take me to a hotel! Any place but here!" Morgan begged.

"Listen, you're really pissing me off. What the fuck are you afraid of?" He parked the car in front of the house.

"Pritchard. That's who I'm afraid of. He said that he will kill me!" Morgan remained in the car, fearing to get out of it.

"Pritchard? We killed his ass over a year ago. He's dead! You don't want to get out of the car, then stay there, I don't give a shit!" Kerry angrily slammed the door and walked into the house.

After an hour of sitting in the car, Morgan accepted his fate. He got out of his car, limped on his makeshift feet, and sat in his wheelchair that Kerry got out of the car, then wheeled himself into the house.

Expecting Trent to return that night to end his misery, he crawled upstairs to his room and laid on his bed, waiting for death to arrive.

Kerry entered his room, apologized for yelling at him in the car, and gave him a huge plateful of fried chicken. Morgan forgave him and said his goodbyes to Kerry because he knew that he wouldn't be alive the next morning. The word got out that Morgan had returned, and all of his brothers and some friends came by his room to see him.

Wyatt, whom many believe maimed Morgan, stopped by as well and reiterated that he didn't do what the others accused him of doing. Morgan believed him because he sensed what had really happened.

Nighttime descended on the Kolb house. Morgan, lying in his bed, didn't know what time it was and didn't care, because he sensed a presence in his room.

"Pritchard, is that you?" he asked, as he sat up in his bed.

Trent, sitting in a chair in the corner, emerged from the shadows, and said, "I am here, Morgan. Welcome back!"

Morgan asked, "Are you going to kill me to-night?"

Trent, amazed that Morgan didn't seem to be as fearful as earlier, said, "Yes, you will die tonight, but if you tell me what I want to know, I will kill you fast. If not, I will inflict as much pain as I can before you die."

"What do you want to know?" Morgan asked.

"You said you recognized a voice other than mine. When did you first hear it?" Trent asked.

"When we kidnapped you. We found out that our father made you his heir and didn't want him to cut us off. We were just fucking around, and that voice told me to kidnap you and put you in the ground. It also told me to shoot you in the back be-fore we put you there. Then after a few months, the voice returned to me and told me to take the police to the spot and to get them to take your body away," he confessed.

"Is that all?" Trent asked.

"We all wondered why we did it after the fact but we didn't know. We held a lot of anger with the Pritchards but we didn't know why. We justified it when we found out that our father visited you, and told you that he was going to leave all his money to you. Without you, the money will go to a trust that our mother set up for us," Morgan confessed.

"Did Ethan kill my parents?"

"No, Kerry and I did. We saw them coming at us on the icy road. The voice came to me again and told me to run them off the road. I felt bad afterward. You said that you will kill me quick if I confessed," Morgan demanded.

"Yes, I will, but here is what I'm going to do. I will stab you in your heart until you are dead and then I will symbolically remove your hands, but only after you're dead so you won't feel any pain. I will do that because my mother is never able to hug me anymore after you killed her. Wyatt will be joining you soon."

"I'm ready, Pritchard. Do the deed. I'm ready!" Morgan said, as he cried like a baby.

Trent removed his knife and buried it deep into Morgan's chest, piercing his heart and killing him instantly and quietly. He removed his hands, but he wasn't done with Morgan's body.

Wyatt slept in his bed, but suddenly awakened when something dripped on his face. He also felt something squeezing his neck.

He reacted in his sleep by trying to remove what pressed on his neck. With his eyes still closed, he felt foreign objects around his neck and woke up. He removed the two objects, but it was dark in the room and he didn't know what he held. With the moonlight shining through an open window, he saw that he held Morgan's two severed hands.

He screamed and threw them aside. "What the fuck?"

He was wide awake, sitting up in his bed, and saw the hands on the floor. He looked at his bed-linens and they were blood red.

There was too much blood for a couple of severed hands. He felt something drip upon his head.

Kerry and Everett ran into Wyatt's room and turned on the lights. They both ran back out when they focused on what had happened in the room. They returned to the room holding their guns pointed above Wyatt.

Looking up, Wyatt saw Morgan's body hanging by his calves, his arms bound together, and missing his hands. Wyatt freaked out, scurried out of bed, and ran as far away as he could from the corpse hanging from the rafters above his bed.

"What the fuck is happening?"

Wyatt screamed as he grabbed his gun thinking that someone must be in his room, "It's Morgan!" He walked nervously toward his dangling brother.

Kerry said frantically, "We know it's Morgan but how the fuck did he get up there? Someone must be in the house."

"Should we cut him down?" asked Everett.

Wyatt, seeing that something was happening within his house beyond his knowledge, said, "No, we have to get the cops involved in this. Call them, Everett."

Retrieving his phone, Everett dialed 911, and told them that someone killed their brother.

The police arrived at the house a half hour later and started an investigation. It was obvious to them that one of the brothers was the culprit.

"You say that the body hung over you when you woke up, Mr. Kolb?" the detective asked Wyatt, as they took Morgan's body down from the ceiling.

"Yes, I felt something around my neck. Someone had cut his hands off and placed them around my neck," Wyatt said, as he explained what he saw.

The detective knew his father was but made no mention of him. He interviewed Kerry and Everett but both had airtight alibis, because they were with women who swore that the brothers were with them. Another detective walked over to the questioning detective and handed him a note. The note read, *You're next, Wyatt!*

He walked back over to Wyatt who sat in a chair in the living room, shaking wildly at what happened to him. "We found this in Morgan's pocket. Does it look like the handwriting of anyone you know?"

Wyatt, seeing the note, said defiantly, "No, I don't know who the fuck wrote this but if he comes after me, I'll kill his ass! I'll be ready for him."

The detective saw Wyatt's arsenal and said, "Do you think one man did this? There are no pulleys to get him up there. That man weighed over two hundred and fifty pounds. Someone lifted him up there and another person had to have tied the knot. How many people are in this house?"

"It's just me and my two brothers and their girlfriends. That's it, as far as I know," Wyatt said.

"We found five pot plants in the house and we're taking those with us," the detective resolved.

"I don't care! Just get his body out of here. I don't know how he got up there or who put him there but I'll sure as fuck find out eventually," Wyatt said, defiantly.

A few hours later, the detective returned to Wyatt.

"Okay, we've interviewed everyone in the house and removed the body and hands. How did Morgan become blind and lose his feet?" the detective asked.

"An accident a few months back. I can't explain how it happened. I saw a sledgehammer dragged across the ground and it raised up by itself and splattered his feet. Three months ago, we found him with his eyes gouged out. We still don't know how that happened and he never told us. Well, he said some ghost did it, but he drank a lot that night so we don't know how it happened," Wyatt explained.

They didn't know that Trent was still in the room, sitting in a chair laughing, unobserved, at Wyatt's bravado knowing that he wouldn't be so brave in a few weeks' time.

Remembering what Morgan told him about the voice, he was convinced that Eli caused his kidnapping, and was the reason he couldn't reenter his own body and possibly reunite with his parents and his beloved Amanda.

He also found out that Eli seemed to have a hand in not only his murder, but also that of his parents and possibly his wife and child as well. There were times when he didn't know who his real enemy was: the Kolb brothers or Eli. The Kolb brothers deserved what they got but he had no way of finding out what he could do to Eli to punish him.

Leaving the house, he met up with Eli, and asked him directly why he wanted him kidnapped and killed as well as his loved ones. Eli didn't answer his questions right away, but said that time had a way of changing things for the worse or better.

"Time and fate conspire to do what they will. We can't change these attributes of life. Shit happens, Trent. We don't travel through life without seeing death and bad things happening. To answer your questions about your family, time destroyed them, not I."

Chapter 17
Wyatt's Fight for Life

Trent didn't want to cause friction between himself and Eli. He needed more answers, and Eli knew those answers but was slow to give them up. Harming a spirit was nearly impossible but there had to be a way, he thought. He wanted to do something about his situation by making Eli go to a place where he would be scared to go, but had forgotten the secret within it, and that was the cave that housed Eli's skeletal remains. Eli appeared to not be afraid of the cave, so Trent suggested that they go there. Eli, always the adventurer, agreed to see the hidden cave, and they immediately walked toward it. They were at the entrance of the cave and Eli appeared to be intrigued about going inside.

"I've been in these woods for decades but I've never seen this cave before. Finally, something that needs to be explored." Eli stepped inside with Trent following behind.

He passed the remains of many miners, but that didn't appear to deter him. They pressed on farther into the cave. In Trent's earlier exploration, he'd found a way to sidestep the room with the bats, as well as the room with Eli's remains. That was the room where he wanted to trap Eli.

After that room, the cave was a dead end, so if he could get Eli in that room without him being suspicious, then he'd have the spirit where he wanted it. Had Eli known what was in the room, he could never enter it because he'd be drawn to his skeletal remains and be absorbed into it, just as Eli said would be Trent's fate should he step over his mortal body and forever be dead. Trent hoped that Eli wouldn't be absorbed right away because he needed more answers to his questions.

He also didn't know the extent of Eli's powers to escape the cave, but it was the only way he could think of, to capture Eli's spirit.

Eli entered the large empty room and asked, "This is amazing! When did you find this place?"

"I found it while I explored the woods but I didn't find it first, you did!" Trent saw confusion on Eli's face.

"I did? I don't remember ever being here."

"Let me show you what I found." Trent led Eli into the next room.

It was pitch black in the room, but that didn't matter to spirits. Trent didn't know that he didn't need light to see.

The first time, he went into the cave blind, but now he'd learned that he could see everything regardless of illumination.

Eli walked into the room, and suddenly hesitated. "I can't go in there, Trent!"

"Why not? What are you afraid of?" he asked, knowing what Eli's concern was.

"I get a feeling that I shouldn't take another step. Why do I feel like this?"

"Is it because you died in that room?"

"No, I died in the woods far away from here… Wait a minute. I did die here the third time," he stated, fearfully.

"The third time? What does that mean, Eli? People don't die a second time much less a third!"

"Trent, I need to get out of here. Now!" Eli appeared agitated.

"Sure, but we have to go through that room to get out."

"No, I can't go through there! There has to be another way! Something's wrong! I can't go through the rocks. My powers. I lost my powers! What the hell is happening in here?"

"Can't you disappear and walk through the rocks?" he asked.

"No, I can't if I'm in this state, I will be drawn straight to my remains. Yes, I did die here and my body is in that room. I can't leave here!" Eli said, with a fear that Trent had never seen before.

"I'm sorry to hear that, but what did you mean that you died for the third time here?" Trent asked, with a smile on his face knowing that he'd trapped Eli.

"I can't tell you that yet. Once the last Kolb brother is dead, then I will be able to tell you everything because then I'll be able to leave these woods forever," Eli confessed.

Trent felt no compassion for the obviously agitated spirit and stated, "I thought that you loved these woods. You told me that many times."

Eli looked around and answered Trent's question. "I did for the first few decades, but until I saw this cave, I thought I had seen everything. I realized after I came here that I've been here before. Do you know another way out of here? My powers are stymied here."

"No, just through that room. When we entered the room, you walked right past your remains and didn't think anything of it," Trent stated, knowing that he and Eli bypassed the room when they entered the adjoining room.

"Wait, you knew that my remains were in here and you brought me anyway? How did you know I'm the one who lay there?"

"Because you wrote your epitaph on the rock wall above your body. My father knew you as 'Patch.' Yes, I know that you were friends with my father and with Randolph Kolb. I also know that you attacked my mother prior to her marrying my father. What did you mean by a prophecy and the sacrifice of five most dear? Never mind, you'll stay here until I get my answers. I'll return when I've dealt with the Kolb brothers."

"Fine, I'll stay here but I will find a way out and will deal with your spirit as I did with your living self. Do you think this cave can hold me? I know things that can hurt you still, even though you're a spirit, and as far as the prophecy, you will never know about that."

Trent didn't think that Eli could do anything, because as he said many times, he needed him to kill the Kolbs. It was all bluster on Eli's part. However, he was sure that Eli could eventually find an alternative route out of the room, so he gathered up Eli's bones and placed them around the room, blocking every exit. Eli couldn't step beyond the bones and he needed to if he wanted to escape the cave.

Trent left the cave knowing that he'd solidly trapped Eli. He went back to the Kolb house to start teaching Wyatt one of his final lessons.

He didn't know what he'd do to the most heinous Kolb brother next to the eldest, Ethan.

Seeing that Wyatt slept with his nine millimeter pistol under his pillow, he simply applied heat to the gun. It glowed red under the pillow and soon the pillow ignited, fully engulfed in flames.

Wyatt woke up with the side of his face on fire. He quickly doused it and removed the pillow to see his gun melting under the extreme heat. Just as he was about to try to get it off his bed, the cartridges fired. One after another, they fired, causing him to flee the room. There were nine cartridges in the magazine and all of them exploded. He managed to elude all the bullets, then walked back into the room and saw that the gun had completely melted on the bed. Strangely, to him, the gun didn't catch the bed on fire as it had his pillow.

Kerry and Everett ran into the room, saw the smoking gun, and asked, "Who are you firing at?"

"I'm not firing at anyone. The gun just melted and then the cartridges exploded."

"Your hair is burned off, Wyatt," informed Kerry.

"I know. I think my ear's burned too. That's the strangest thing I've ever seen."

"You think this is part of what Morgan said about you being next?" Kerry asked.

Wyatt, for the first time, thought that he might not have taken the death of Morgan as seriously as he should have.

He was convinced that someone entered his home and murdered his brother, but seeing his gun glow red for no reason caused him to be concerned for his safety. It was midnight and Wyatt was tired, but he wasn't about to go to sleep in the house. It was eighty degrees outside but he thought it better to sleep in a tent. Kerry and Everett slept outside as well. The Kolbs didn't know what was happening to them but the town loved the fact that they didn't visit it to cause havoc among its citizens. Trent loved the fact that he made strides to keep the town's citizens safe.

Wyatt grabbed a few beers and his CD player and blasted some old George Jones music as he sat on his chair outside the tent. A young girl entered the tent and Wyatt finished off a beer and followed her inside. "Who are you, sweet thing, and where did you come from?" he asked, as she sat down.

Her bright blue eyes turned black and calmly declared, "I'm here to kill you, silly boy."

"Kill me? I don't think a little thing like you could kill me unless you're talking about killing me by fucking me," he said with a laugh.

"That's exactly what I meant, Wyatt. You want to get to it?" she asked.

Wyatt grabbed her hair, pulled her toward him, and started licking her neck while he ripped her clothes off.

Moving her into position, he took his shorts off, and started having sex as Kerry came in his tent. "What the fuck are you doing, Wyatt?"

"What does it look like I'm doing? I'm fucking this girl," he replied, as he continued thrusting.

"That's a car battery you fucking, dumbass," Kerry informed him as he chuckled at the sight.

Wyatt looked down. His penis was stuck in an acid-filled car battery. He pulled it out, and it blistered and bled badly. He grabbed his beer and poured it on himself but the pain was too intense. He stood up and ran into the woods to a nearby stream. He splashed around for a half an hour before he stood still, and wondered about the extent of the damage he did to himself. He sustained a serious injury but soon he realized that piranhas infested the thigh-deep water he waded in. They swarmed and ravaged his legs. He struggled and managed to reach the shore with hundreds of the hungry fish attached to both of his legs. He saw that the flesh-eating fish gnawed his legs to the bone. He couldn't walk and yelled for Kerry or Everett to help but they didn't heed his cries. He looked at the red water and saw the remnants of a mass of skin devoured by the voracious eaters amid the turbulent water.

A minute later, as he sat on the bank in anguish, he noticed that the water was calm and saw Trent walking slowly out of it toward him.

"Who are you?" he asked, while grasping his injured legs.

"I'm the guy who's going to kill you Wyatt. Remember me? I'm Trent Pritchard and you killed me, so I'm here to return the favor," he imparted in a calm, haunting voice.

"Fuck you, asshole!" he said, as he threw a rock right through Trent. "What the fuck are you? A ghost? I need a doctor, dammit!"

"I think I can help you out." Trent snapped his fingers. Wyatt was instantly in a white operating room lying on a strange, stainless steel table with grooves down the center. Arms and legs tied down, he wore a white hospital gown.

"Where am I?" he asked, as he tried to wrestle himself free. He noticed that his legs were intact but he was more concerned as to how Trent instantly sent him to the room.

A doctor walked in, or, he assumed that he was a doctor considering his white smock. Wyatt demanded that he release him.

The doctor ignored him as he brought over a blue velvet case. He untied it, opened it up, and Wyatt saw many very sharp and shiny instruments.

"What are those for?" he asked, but the doctor didn't acknowledge his question.

"Hey, I'm talking to you, asshole!"

The doctor removed Wyatt's hospital gown. He laid there stark naked on the table at the total mercy of the doctor. The doctor had a nametag which read Dr. Babe Ruth.

"Babe Ruth? Are you serious?" he asked, but again, the doctor refused to answer him.

Wyatt saw that he took out his scalpel and positioned it at his collarbone. Wyatt panicked. "What the fuck are you doing?"

He watched in horror as the doctor cut him deep and followed his collarbone to his breastbone, but it didn't hurt him. He struggled to get loose but he couldn't. The doctor continued cutting him from the other side of his collarbone and that incision met the other one. Then he continued to cut him from his neck to his navel.

Viewing his own autopsy, Wyatt bellowed as loud as he could, "I'm not dead, you asshole!"

The doctor stopped cutting and screamed, "I know that you're not dead but you will be soon. I'm going to gut you like a deer. I've allowed you the courtesy of you not feeling this but since you insist on moving, I think that I'll change that."

Trent snapped his fingers and the pain that Wyatt felt seared through his mind as he saw the doctor pull out a sternum saw.

He turned it on. Wyatt winced in extreme pain as the doctor sawed right down his breast, separating his ribs. Wyatt opened his eyes as tears rained down and he saw his beating heart.

Removing a lung the doctor placed it in a bucket. Blood seeped out of Wyatt's mouth as he lay there, helpless. His eyes had a terrorized look as he suffered with every organ removal. The man removed his heart but he still saw what the doctor did to him and still felt intense pain. The pain finally got to him and he passed out.

***

*A*n hour later, he woke up in the tent, sweating profusely. He looked at his legs and his penis to find out that he'd dreamed the whole experience.

He walked out of the tent and took a deep breath, happy that it was just a dream. He felt an itch on his chest and saw a scar. He removed his shirt and saw the doctor's incisions and staples used to close up the wounds. "What the fuck?"

His brothers came running and saw his chest but they didn't see the autopsy scars and thought that Wyatt was drunk. "There's nothing wrong with your chest. Get a grip, Wyatt!" Kerry declared.

Wyatt put his shirt back on and realized that there were no scars, but the dream was still vivid in his mind. Kerry left the tent and went over to where he and Everett were drinking with a few friends.

Wyatt, not being in the mood to drink, re-entered his tent to see the same cute little girl he saw in his dream.

"Not this time, bitch!"

Slapping her across the face, he sent her flying across the tent. Groggy, she got to her feet and held her face as she ran from the tent crying loudly and ran back to where the small party continued.

Kerry, seeing the girl leave with a few of her friends, asked her, "What the hell happened?"

"Your deranged brother hit me in the face for just being in his tent! I'm leaving."

She disclosed what happened to her girlfriends and they assisted her to her car.

Kerry ran back over to Wyatt's tent, jumped inside, and asked, "Why the fuck did you hit her? I sent her over here to relax you and you hit her in the face?"

"She's not real, Kerry! I saw her in my dream and as I fucked her, she turned into a car battery and that's where it began. I'm not going down that road again!" he stated, definitively.

Kerry, not believing what he'd heard, said, "Damn, you have got some serious issues, bro."

Storming out of the tent, Kerry went back over to his party, and left Wyatt to wonder what was happening to him. Wyatt laid down on his cot and hoped to fall asleep quickly and put an end to the night that haunted him.

Chapter 18
Wyatt's Defiance

In his thoughts were Morgan and Ethan as he drifted off. He awoke suddenly and saw a shadowy figure sitting in the chair across from his cot in his huge tent, but it wasn't Trent.

"Who's there?" he inquired. His query went unanswered. Wyatt jumped up and pointed a shotgun at the man sitting in the chair.

"Put the gun down, Wyatt. It will do you no good because I'm not really here," the familiar voice disclosed, as the figure arose. Wyatt saw that it was Ethan, his long-dead older brother. "You're dead! It can't be you!"

Wyatt continued to point his shotgun at the vision. Ethan, irritated, raised his hand and the shotgun shed parts until Wyatt held just the stock.

"Why are you here, Ethan?" he asked, as he threw the stock aside.

"I'm here because you called me here and I came. I will die in the spirit world, but I needed to help you because you will die soon and I don't want you to be afraid of it. I didn't come to Morgan when he called. There are some things you need to know. First off, we weren't supposed to be born."

"Bullshit, Ethan, if that's who you really are."

"Listen to me, asshole, we're here because of the intervention of a spirit. I can't fix that, nor can I do much to protect you, as I've not lived a stellar life. I killed over twenty souls in my short lifetime and altered their existence so I'm paying for that mistake now," he confessed, as he strolled around the tent.

"What do you want me to do about it?" Wyatt expressed with contempt.

"I want you to take your shotgun and place the barrel in your mouth and pull the trigger," he explained, as the shotgun magically floated in front of him and reassembled itself.

"You're fucking crazy! I'm not going to do that!" He spouted, "Why should I do that?"

Ethan's ghostly image explained, "It's because you're being tortured by Pritchard. You'll die a terrible, painful death and I want to spare you that. You were my favorite brother and I don't want you to go through that."

Defiant, Wyatt stated, "I will fight whoever or whatever tries to kill me!"

"You cannot win this fight. You will die. Fate is correcting an error made by a rogue spirit. You can't fight fate. I can thwart one attack from Pritchard, then I will die again and never come back. As I said before, we were never supposed to be born, so you should accept death when it comes. There is no after-life for us," Ethan sadly imparted the grim news as he drifted away.

Waking up again with his dream still vivid in his mind, Wyatt wondered about what the spirit of Ethan said but was thankful that he would protect him once.

Trent was unaware of Ethan's interference, and Wyatt was counting on that, because he had a plan should Trent show up and torture him. He knew that he couldn't fight him, but hoped to create doubt in Trent's resolve that Wyatt had no chance of survival. He wasn't totally convinced about all that he'd experienced, but he was quick to accept that Morgan died mysteriously, and he remembered that sledgehammer that magically dragged itself toward a blind Morgan. He didn't have long to wait because Trent came to him outside his tent carrying a long razor-sharp sword.

"I decided to make this quick, asshole!" Trent pronounced, as he approached Wyatt.

"Give me all you got. You can't touch me!" Wyatt boasted, as he defiantly stood up to the spirit. "Pritchard, I have powers as well. You can't harm me!"

Trent didn't know what he talked about and thrust the sword into his heart.

Shockingly, Wyatt saw the sword had completely impaled him, and he laughed at Trent as he pulled the sword out of his body and swung it wildly at Trent, sending it through his spirit's body.

Wyatt threw the sword aside and said, "Is that all you got? I told you, you cannot harm me; now go away and don't come back because I can destroy you if you try."

Wyatt knew that he possessed no such power, but used Ethan's lone protective curse to attempt to make Trent believe that he was untouchable and could possibly thwart future attacks.

Trent stepped back and wondered who Wyatt was and why his sword didn't kill him. Scared, he retreated to figure out how Wyatt did what he did. He needed to talk to Eli before he proceeded further because he wasn't used to a living being thwarting his attacks.

***

Walking into the cave and through the bat-laden room, and into the room where he saw a surly Eli sitting on a rock.

"I tried to kill Wyatt. I put a two-foot sword right through him and he pulled it out and threw it at me. The sword didn't hurt him at all. How is that possible?" Trent asked.

"It's impossible unless he's getting help from the spirit world. If I had been there, it wouldn't have happened. You need me, especially if the spirit world is trying to stop you. You've trapped me here and I can't move. I saw what you did with my bones, very clever."

Eli threw a rock across his leg bone and into the empty chasm of the cave.

"I'm not thoroughly convinced that you're not my enemy. You talk in riddles and espouse the benefits of being in the woods, and then complain that you've been there for too long. Which is it?"

"Okay, Trent, I'm reluctant to tell you because it means that you won't go through with your plan. I've told you that time means nothing in our world; however, we can alter time to change things. I confess that I'm guilty of attempting to change what time wrought on me as a young child, but I'm not prepared to tell you why I did it. When you kill the last Kolb brother, I will tell you everything I've done. Keeping me here will not get the answers you require any faster."

Venturing closer to the exit, Eli tested the barrier that Trent created. He continued, "Wyatt had help but in doing so, destroyed someone's chances of going further in the afterlife. It could have been Morgan or even Ethan who came back to protect him, but they have a limited amount of power and after they have left, Wyatt is again susceptible to whatever you have planned for him."

Trent, angered at Wyatt's attempt to deceive him, ran back to the house to see him sleeping soundly in his tent, so he set it on fire, readying himself for when he emerged.

Wyatt woke up with his legs on fire and ran out of the blazing tent, dropped to the ground, and patted his still burning legs.

"Your brother's spirit stopped me last time but it can't do it again. I will kill you tonight and it will be painful. I won't allow you to die until you feel the kind of pain that you've inflicted on the innocents in your sorry, drunken life," Trent explained.

Smoke and fumes from the flames of the burning tent outlined his spiritual form. The fire dissipated and Wyatt saw that he was face-to-face with a spirit hell-bent on ending his days on earth. Wyatt limped into the house but there was nowhere to run. Trent followed him and simply waved his hand, and Wyatt's leg snapped in half.

Wincing in agonizing pain, he begged Trent to have mercy on him but there was no mercy in his eyes as he snapped the other leg. Wyatt screamed for help and his brothers as well as the rest of his friends came running.

They arrived to see Wyatt hovering above them with both legs broken in multiple places. They looked in amazement as he begged his brothers to help him.

Kerry stepped away and yelled, "What the fuck are you doing up there? How is that possible?"

Trent swiped Wyatt away with an easy wave of his hand, which sent him crashing into a wall, looked at Kerry and said, "You will be next, Kerry, but for right now, I'm not done with this idiot so watch and see what you'll experience soon."

Raising Wyatt in the air, he snapped his right arm with a simple flick of his fingers. The group couldn't move as Trent's gaze made them stay and watch as he continued torturing Wyatt with the breaking of his other arm. Wyatt was in extraordinary pain but still conscious, and while he was, Trent made him spin. Slowly at first, but steadily faster, Wyatt's broken body spun. Eventually, it spun so fast that the inertial force generated from him spinning ripped his four limbs from his body and catapulted them through walls of the house.

Trent dropped his bloody torso in front of Kerry and said, "I stopped him because I want you to see what he's become with his final breaths."

Wyatt amazingly opened his eyes, and mumbled words to Kerry.

Kerry didn't hear Wyatt's words, but Trent felt better showing his next victim what was to become of him. Wyatt bled to death seconds after Trent threw him onto the living room floor. Trent released Kerry and his friends and they ran as fast as they could away from the bloody mayhem within the house.

Kerry and Everett were the only brothers left, but Kerry was the more scared because Wyatt mumbled that he was next just before he died.

"What are we going to do, Kerry?" asked Everett.

"How the fuck do I know? You were friends with Pritchard, can you talk him out of attacking us?"

"Are you joking? Did you see what he did to Morgan and Wyatt? Trent is not the same guy I knew. We could apologize to him for killing his family."

"No fucking way! We did what we did because they're all assholes!" said Kerry.

"I think we should burn the house down and take over Dad's home. Trent's not familiar with the inside of that. Besides, Dad's got hidden rooms in that house," suggested Everett.

"Now, that's a great idea! Except our old man would just as soon put a bullet in us rather than let us live there," Kerry asserted.

Everett suggested, "The house is so big, maybe we can take over one side of the house. He'd never know that we're there."

Kerry agreed.

***

That night, Trent observed the two brothers dousing their house with gasoline and igniting it into great walls of flames.

Trent didn't know what the remaining Kolb brothers had in mind by torching their house, but he speculated that they surmised that the house was what brought the terror to their doorstep.

Just as Trent was about to leave, something strange happened. Kerry, mesmerized by the massive fire, began walking toward it. Trent ran to Kerry as he walked and asked him what he was doing. Kerry didn't speak and acted as if he was in a trance. Trent tried to stop him from walking, but his feet never stopped moving.

Trent wouldn't have his revenge taken from him so he broke Kerry's legs.

He fell to the ground immediately but showed no indication of pain and crawled toward the fire.

Trent knew that there could only be one reason for Kerry's desire to be in the fire. Eli was making him commit suicide. Trent saw that it would take a while before Kerry reached the fire, so he instantly returned to the cave to confront Eli.

"Are you making Kerry walk into that fire?" Trent asked.

"Nope, remember? I can't kill them. Besides, I have no powers here while those bones are blocking my path. Whoever is doing it, I applaud them. Perhaps, the recently deceased Wyatt is using his one and only power to end his brother's life to deprive you of that opportunity," Eli said with a smile.

Trent returned to the burning house, entered into Kerry's body, and saw that Eli was correct. Wyatt's spirit implored Kerry to walk into the fire. Trent had to break the spirit's will because he wanted to use the final two brothers to get more answers out of Eli.

However, just as Ethan's final power helped Wyatt when Trent drove that sword through his heart, he couldn't thwart the last power of a spirit. Everett sat back and watched as Kerry crawled all the way to the fire. He couldn't move as he saw Kerry's head catch fire and still he crawled all the way into the fire despite Trent's efforts to make him stop. Soon, he was fully engulfed in flames, stood up and faced Everett, then suddenly crumpled into dust.

Trent left the inferno and went back to the cave.

Snapping out of his trance, Everett ran to where he saw Kerry walk into the fire, but there was nothing he could do. Kerry was dead and Wyatt got the last laugh on Trent.

He had one more brother to torment but he wasn't about to torture and kill his last means of getting answers from Eli.

He vowed not to kill Everett until he got what he needed but he had to protect against Kerry's last spiritual power to do the same to Everett. Trent snapped his fingers and the fire was doused instantly with absolutely no residual smoke so Everett was not tempted to walk into it as Kerry had done.

Trent decided to have a talk with his old friend Everett. He appeared to him and made a deal. Trent told him that he'd had no involvement in Kerry's death and that in the spiritual world, a recently departed spirit receives one power before he finally leaves the mortal coil.

Trent told him that he'd spare his life if he refused the spirit of Kerry asking him to do something that he wouldn't ordinarily do.

Trent didn't know if Everett possessed the ability to resist the spirit because, apparently, Kerry couldn't. Trent told him to follow him back to the cave, because he couldn't be in two places at one time. Trent placed him in a trance and Everett followed him without question.

They returned to the cave and walked to where Trent trapped Eli.

They walked in the room.

Eli stood up and asked excitedly, "Why did you bring him here? Dammit!"

"I brought him here to protect him."

"Protect him? Kill him! Kill him now!" Eli demanded.

Trent didn't understand why Eli reacted the way he did but after Trent released his trance, he shockingly found out.

Everett shook his head and frantically looked all around. He was in a dark cave and couldn't see anything.

Eli immediately tried to go invisible but being in the presence of his human remains, he held no power to do so. Trent saw that Everett couldn't see and lit a torch, which temporarily blinded Everett. He covered his eyes, then once his eyes focused, he looked and was face-to-face with a very worried Eli.

Everett looked at Eli and asked something that shocked Trent. "Dad? Is that you, Dad?"

Trent interrupted and asked, "Did you say dad?"

Everett turned around, saw Trent, and backed away, tripping over rocks, thinking that he was going to kill him as he did all his brothers.

"Don't kill me, Trent," he begged.

"I told you! I will not kill you, Everett! I need answers and by the reaction of Eli here, I'm about to get them."

Trent helped Everett to his feet. "Is this your father? I thought Randolph Kolb was your father."

"He's my stepfather. I just found out a few years ago. He married my real mother who married that man over there," Everett said, still fearful that Trent would kill him.

"He's lying, Trent! I'm not his father!" Eli insisted.

"Ethan showed me pictures but he is much younger in them. He looks like my father. I was only two years old when he left us.

I never regarded him as my father, but my mother confessed just before she died more than five years ago."

Eli angrily responded, "I tell you he's lying! Why would I want to kill my own kids, Trent? Think about it! Who goaded you into killing the Kolbs?"

"You did, but according to the obituary you scrolled above your remains, you have five children. Where are they?" Trent asked.

"I don't know! I've been dead for decades. The last I knew, they were in New Jersey and I have three daughters and two sons, not five sons!"

Everett stepped back and began to run but Trent stopped him and made him walk back. Shocked, he asked, "You two are dead? Are either of you going to kill me?"

Trent assured him that he wouldn't and also stated, "Eli is stuck here. He's my captive and he possesses no powers while he's here.

So, he can't touch you as long as this leg bone is here in front of him."

"I don't want to be here! I need to sit down or I'm going to fall down!" Everett began to shake uncontrollably due to fear of what he saw.

Trent allowed him to sit but the torch flickered and suddenly extinguished and they were completely in the dark. Everett couldn't see Trent or Eli and he panicked.

Trent was worried that the young man was going to have a heart attack because of his circumstances. He also knew that he'd have to supply food and water to keep him alive. He was finally receiving answers but he needed more from Everett and Eli.

Chapter 19
The Death of a Titan

Two days went by and both Everett and Eli were silent.

Trent saw that Everett weakened and needed food and drink, but he wasn't about to allow him to go out and get something; besides, he was too weak to make it to a place to eat. Trent was also not about to take Everett away because he was fearful that the spirit of Kerry would use his one remaining power to kill him, and he thought that the cave was a safe haven to keep that from happening. Eli possessed no power to make Everett kill himself, so he decided to leave the cave on his own to hunt a deer and gather some water from a nearby stream.

Trent left the cave after placing Everett in a trance to ensure he stayed put.

However, the trance didn't prevent him from speaking with Eli. When Trent left, Eli went into action. He stood up, called for Everett, and tried to fool him into thinking that Trent was their real enemy.

"Everett, I'm sorry that I told Trent that I'm not your father, but I had to, to save your life. You are the youngest and I remember taking you home from the hospital. Your mother and I felt so proud. Trent is a killer spirit. He killed your brothers. You know that! I need you to do something for me. I promise you that I will protect you, but I can't while I'm here. Can I count on you?" Eli asked.

"Yes, father, you can. Trent killed my brothers but he made them suffer too. What do you want me to do?" asked Everett.

The two had a discussion as Trent hunted and easily killed a deer, dressed it, and removed enough meat to keep Everett alive for another week or two. He also grabbed five gallons of water from a nearby stream and easily carried the load back to the cave.

Walking back to where he'd trapped Eli, he saw him sitting in the corner but Everett had vanished.

Looking down to ensure that the leg bones were still there in front of Eli, he was convinced that the trance he placed on Everett hadn't been strong enough to hold him.

"Where is he, Eli?" Trent put down the meat and water.

"How the hell do I know? I'm stuck here! He left on his own," Eli muttered, as he turned his back on Trent.

"I'll find him!" Trent exclaimed, as he disappeared.

He searched where Everett's house burned to the ground, but Everett wasn't there, so he went to town to the Balls Bluff Tavern and noticed that the place was abuzz with the latest news that someone murdered Randolph Kolb fifteen minutes earlier and that Everett Kolb was the prime suspect. They also uttered to each other that Everett had eaten and left the establishment recently. Trent didn't converse with the people there but from what he gathered, Everett quietly ate and left without paying, a normal occurrence for the Kolbs. When the people stopped Everett, he threw a twenty-dollar bill on the floor, so the people who held him released him and he slowly walked out.

Trent immediately went back to the cave as Everett walked in. Trent talked to him but he didn't answer him immediately, because he was still in the slight trance that Trent placed on him. He walked back to where Eli was. Everett sat on a rock, noticed the deer meat, and began eating it raw.

Trent immediately removed the trance and Everett gagged when he saw what he was eating.

"Everett, where did you go?" asked Trent.

"I didn't go anywhere! I stayed right here," he revealed.

Angered, he lifted Everett all the way to the top of the cave, twenty feet above them.

Everett begged him not to drop him and cried and yelled that he hadn't left the cave. Suddenly, he confessed, and Trent allowed him to gently return to the cave's floor.

"I want answers! I'm not fucking around with you, Everett! Did you kill Randolph Kolb? Yes or no?" Trent asked, as Eli looked on.

"Yes, I killed him. I shot him in the head. I needed to kill him!" Everett revealed, calmly.

Trent asked, "Why? Why did you kill him?"

"I hated him. I've always hated him," Everett imparted in a monotone voice.

Noticing his demeanor was similar to being in a trance, he knew that he wasn't the only one controlling Everett. However, he also knew that Eli couldn't use his powers because his barren leg bone was still in front of him. He asked Eli anyway, but he didn't utter a word but offered a wry smile. Trent felt sorry for Randolph Kolb's death because he knew that he was a good man and thought back to his conversation with him, as well as his father's thoughts on the man.

"Where did you get the gun, Everett?"

"At my house. We had guns hidden in the woods. I have one more to go!" he asserted, as Eli stood up and acted concerned at Everett's announcement.

"One more? What do you mean by that?" Eli walked toward Everett and seemed worried about him answering the question.

Everett immediately shut up, not paying attention to Trent either, and then, just as suddenly, fell asleep right there on the rocks.

"Are you doing this, Eli?" Trent asked.

"How can I do anything? You trapped me! Remember?" Eli pointed toward the leg bone. "Everett has been awake for nearly three days, his body just shut down."

Trent allowed him to sleep; he wanted him well rested because he felt that he was very close to learning the truth.

***

Trent felt obligated to attend Randolph's funeral a few days later. Just to be sure, he tied up Everett and didn't allow him to leave the cave.

Trent disappeared, and reappeared at the cemetery. Very few people showed up to attend the services, but his father's old friend Remy was there to read passages as they lowered Randolph into the vault and sealed it. Trent saw that Remy was emotional, given that he was the last of the Lost River Boys.

Trent was behind him as he walked away from Randolph's grave. He could do nothing to help the grieving man, but Janie was there for Remy, and Trent was thankful for that.

Trent walked to the graves of his parents, sat down, and said, "Dad, I really need you now. I hope that I'll be with you soon but I don't know how yet. Give a kiss to Mom and to Amanda for me. I'm working my way to all of you."

He kissed the newly rebuilt Amanda's monument and then appeared at his own grave nearby, but was shocked to see that someone had dug it up, the top of the vault ajar and his casket busted open with his decomposing body exposed. He immediately collapsed and crawled away from the grave. His powers were nonexistent so he depended on his legs to get away from his decomposed body. Far enough away, he stood up and disappeared, knowing that his powers returned to him. Something was amiss and he knew that somehow Eli was behind it. He reappeared at Randolph's grave to see Remy and Janie walking hand-in-hand to their car.

Suddenly, from behind a tree, a mud-soaked Everett walked toward Remy and pointed a gun at him. Trent instinctively stepped in front of Remy as Everett pumped three shots into Trent's chest. The bullets passed through Trent and penetrated Remy's chest, killing him instantly.

"Everett, go back to the cave! Dammit! How did you get loose?" Trent questioned.

"Prophecy number three about to be fulfilled," he said as he placed the gun to his head.

"No! Everett! I command you to put the gun down!"

Everett didn't toss the gun aside.

The people at the ceremony had long left, so there was no one there but Trent, Everett, and Janie.

"I must fulfill the prophecy," Everett stated, as he pulled the trigger. However, the gun was out of cartridges but he continued pulling the trigger anyway.

Raising his hand, Trent walked with him back to the cave. Everett walked slowly and it seemingly took forever but Trent didn't allow him out of his sight. He needed to get him back and hidden before the authorities caught up to him. He felt sorrow that he had to leave Janie there with her fallen husband, but things just got too serious to stay any longer. He was convinced that Eli was doing this but he didn't know how.

Arriving at the cave, Trent picked up the leg bone and moved it closer to Eli as he cowered backward and begged Trent to back off.

"What are you doing, Trent?"

Trent was in no mood for games. "I'm going to either get answers from you or you're going back to hell."

"What do you want to know?" Eli stared at the bone in Trent's hand.

"I want to know about the prophecies!"

"Okay! Okay! Just get that away from me! I died at twelve years old in a field in the mountains. The same spot where your father and I went hunting all the time. I know I shouldn't have been there, but your father drowned the year before..."

Trent interrupted. "My father didn't die! You should know because you pulled him out of the water! Besides, I'm here! How do you reconcile that?"

"No, he did die. Please, let me finish! Where was I? Oh, as I said, I hunted up in the mountains and broke my leg. I remember being in extreme pain and couldn't move. I sat there for two weeks and knew that no one would find me. Your father was the only person alive who could have found me but, as I said, he drowned a year earlier. Near death, I begged God to help me but no help was evident so I made a pledge to the devil that he could have my soul if he helped me. A strange voice came to me and said that he could help me. He said that he'll allow me to go back in time to when Ben was thrown in the water and save him so he could save me in the field up on that mountain," he explained. Trent backed away, to Eli's delight.

Trent believed what Eli said because he still didn't know the extent of a spirit's power.

Thus far, Eli's story seemed plausible but he needed to know more before he completely believed him.

"You can go back in time?" he asked.

"Yes, we as spirits can go back one time, but I didn't know that at the time, because I still lived. We can only go back and affect time if we were there before. In other words, myself, Jordy, Ben and Margie, Randolph, and Remy were the only ones who could possibly go back and affect time because we were the only ones there at the pond," he explained.

Trent interrupted a few times but Eli asked him to wait until he finished before he asked questions.

Eli continued, "So, I accepted the dark spirit's offer but I had to see to it that five people dear to me perished, but not by my hand. I remember being mere minutes away from death. I accepted the offer and instantly died. No one ever found my body, because the wolves dragged my carcass off and ate me. I watched as they tore my flesh apart and licked my bones. I lived the next sixty years as a spirit before the dark spirit granted my wish. As a spirit, I saw my friends live out the rest of their days in perfect harmony and I longed to live my life the way they did.

"Tell me about my mother. What happened to her?" Trent asked, as he sat down and listened to the fantastic story.

"She married Randolph and had three children, two girls and a boy. They lived an idyllic life of wealth and happiness. They died in their eighties not ten days apart."

"What about Amanda, the pastor's daughter?" Trent inquired.

"You mean your wife? She married and also lived a genuinely happy life in Raleigh, North Carolina," he replied.

"What about the Kolb brothers?"

Eli replied, "They were never there because Randolph married your mother instead of my ex-wife, the mother of the Kolb brothers and my sons."

Trent felt happy and sad at the same time. Happy because everyone he loved lived a happy life, but sad because he wasn't a part of it. "So what happened next?"

"Suddenly, the prophesy took hold and propelled me back in time with all my friends on the side of Glover's pond. Old man Glover surprised us and we all ran—except Ben. Glover caught him and angrily threw him in the pond. Ben went down to the bottom instantly and tangled in some underwater branches. Glover jumped in but couldn't get him free of the branches. Glover left in a great hurry and I jumped in and saved him. A year later, Ben led a search party to find me because he had a good idea of my location. I saved Ben so he would save me. That was not to be the end of my hell on earth."

"So, if it wasn't for your journey back, my father would have died and I wouldn't have been born?" questioned Trent.

"That's right! You wouldn't have been born because your father died as a child," Eli explained.

Trent, depressed and not knowing what to think of what he'd learned, tried to reconcile his existence but couldn't. It was tough to believe Eli but he felt confident that he told the truth.

"You said that you had to sacrifice five people dear to you. Who did you sacrifice?" Trent inquired placing the leg bone on the cave floor in front of him.

"I don't want to talk about that! It is a very painful time in my life!" said Eli, with his head low.

Trent picked up the bone and moved it closer to Eli.

Eli opened up, “Okay! I killed my parents and my sisters!”

“You did what? I thought you said that you couldn’t do the deed,” Trent asked, as he lowered the bone again.

Chapter 20
Eli Explains

"I didn't kill them directly. My father spilled gasoline all over the back porch. I invited my friend over who smoked, and we went to the back porch and I watched as he put out his cigarette out on the wood. It went up in flames so fast that my family wasn't able to get out fast enough and they perished. So, I fulfilled the prophecy by killing five most dear, and I lived. If I didn't do what I did, you wouldn't be here. I'm not proud of what I did but I wanted to live!" Eli disclosed.

"You were a despicable human being and an equally disgusting spirit," he angrily retorted.

"It's self-preservation, Trent. I wanted to live a full life," he selfishly replied.

"That's not living a happy life knowing that you killed your family to reach that end. Everett spoke of multiple prophecies and you just spoke of one," he questioned.

"I had to invoke it again when I turned twenty-two and a car struck me in New Jersey. My wife had just given birth to our fifth child, Everett here. I had to do what I did because I wanted to see my children grow up and be with them rather than overseeing them in spirit form. I don't know why I'd been given the gift to return over and over again, but I am certainly going to use it."

"Five more people had to be killed, right?" Trent asked.

"That's right. I had to sacrifice five more people most dear to satisfy the new prophecy, but as I said earlier, I couldn't be the one who did it. For reasons unknown to me, the prophecy propelled me back and I avoided the car crash. I moved my family back to Red Dirt that year, thinking it would be safer there and the town's people welcomed me with open arms. Randolph allowed my family to stay at his estate until I got reestablished in the community, but a prophecy had to be paid and my old gang—Ben, Remy, Randolph, and Jordy—were selected to pay it."

"That's only four. Who is the fifth?" he asked.

"Your mother was the fifth because I loved her more than life itself, but she didn't return my affection. My friends were so well liked in the community that I found it difficult because there was no one to kill my friends, so it took quite a while to find someone to fulfill the prophecy," he confessed.

Trent, seething with anger, asked, "If there were a way to kill you right now, I would. I will sell my soul to the devil if you stood alive right here in front of me so I could squeeze the life out of you! Who did you find to kill them?"

Eli pointed to Everett.

Trent, still angry, asked, "You got your kids to kill them? You bred your children to be killers?"

"I had to! They took an extraordinarily long time to do it because they only cared about drinking and causing mayhem. Eventually, they did what I bred them to do, though. Which brings me to why my remains are here in this cave. I left my family for an excursion in the woods and thousands of bats attacked me. They made quick work of me, so I called for one more prophecy, the last one before I descended to hell. However, with the new prophecy, five more people had to die. I went missing for a year. My wife said that I abandoned them and later, she married Randolph and he adopted my children. When they got old enough, they'd see my last prophecy through."

"Did they kill Jordy as well?" he asked, getting more disgusted the more he heard.

"Ethan took exception at being thrown out of the bar and Jordy confronted him at the house. Ethan shot and killed him. Morgan killed your mother and father. Morgan and Kerry abducted you and Everett took care of Randolph and Remy. They were taught well."

Not wanting to hear any more, he threw the leg bone down in front of Eli and disappeared. Eli, amused to see Trent so angry, laughed as Trent dispersed.

Trent reappeared at the cemetery in front of his beloved wife's grave and whispered, "I wish to give you back what he took from you, sweetheart. I will find a way. Eli will not win and you will be back. I promise you."

Trent spent the whole afternoon going from grave to grave thinking about all that he'd lost in a single lifetime and all that they had lost. He searched for ideas to make things right but nothing came to mind.

Easily, he could send Eli back to death by simply throwing the leg bone at him and have it come into contact with him, but that wouldn't make things right. The people who Eli had killed deserved a life as well.

Stopping Eli and his evil desire to live when fate had already dealt death to him three times, was his new focus.

Ten good people died to make sure he lived, but Trent thought that there was more to the story. He felt reasonably calm after having private conversations with the tombstones and was ready to get the rest of the story. He also wondered how he could affect time since Eli told him that in spirit form, he could invoke it one time. He spoke to the heavens but got no response. He certainly wouldn't take lives to exact his revenge.

Trent wasn't concerned about living anymore. He just wanted to stop Eli from enacting his own form of immortality.

To do so, he had to know the rest of his evil plan, so he reappeared at the cave.

He walked up to the smiling spirit and asked, "The third prophecy? What is the third prophecy?" he asked, as he wondered why Eli was so easily telling him what happened.

"The third prophecy is the result of my dying in this hellhole of a cave. My friends were dead, my parents and sisters were dead, so the only five I could think of were my sons, and who would be the perfect one to kill them? You! I had Morgan kidnap and kill you to bring you to my world.

"You had already dispatched Ethan. I felt that you'd exact your revenge and thus, unknowingly, fulfill my destiny for me. I knew how angry you were at my sons and that you'd kill them given the opportunity.

"I also knew that you couldn't go back in time to change what I changed because if you did, that meant that you'd never be born. It is the perfect paradox, wouldn't you say? Now with Everett here killing Remy and Randolph, there are no more alive that day at the pond and thus you can't reverse it. There is one last task to perform, and that is for Everett here to be killed, and I will come back as a twenty-four-year-old very rich man."

"Rich? How will you be rich?" Trent asked.

"Simple. You see, Randolph left everything he owned to you. However, because of your untimely death, his estate reverted back to its original heirs, the Lost River Boys. They're all dead, but I didn't die. Once I've recovered my life, I will simply walk back in town and receive my rewards. There's only one thing in my way and that's the boy over there. Once he's dead, then the prophecy will be completed and I will walk out of here and into my new life as the richest man in the state."

"It's that easy for you? To just kill your last son for your own salvation?"

"Oh, I won't kill him and neither will you because, quite frankly, knowing what you know, you wouldn't do it anyway. There's no doubt that Janie has gone to the authorities and told them that Everett murdered Remy in cold blood. I think I'll let the state of West Virginia do that for me," he speculated.

Trent smiled and was surprised that Eli didn't allow for the slowness of the state to prosecute murderers.

"You'll have a long wait for that to happen. One year to go to trial, another year for the trial, and ten years to wait on death row. By the time the state executes Everett, your money will have been dispersed to the state or his distant heirs and you'll be declared dead," Trent explained.

Eli knew he was right, and now, he needed Trent more than ever.

A young man, Everett could live a long time without intervention, and Trent wasn't about to hasten his demise.

Eli stood up and disappeared. Trent was in shock to see that Eli had used his powers when he thought that he couldn't. He turned around to see Eli behind him. Trent walked over to him and grabbed the leg bone but Eli just smiled and took it from him. The bone had no effect on him as he threw it aside.

"Perhaps you should have walked through the cave rather than just appearing, for if you had, you would have seen that a leg bone from one of the miners is missing! I convinced my son here to switch them out, so I'm free from my prison. However, the cell will not be empty."

Eli raised up an arm bone that still possessed much of the flesh on it, which he had gotten Everett to retrieve from Trent's grave.

Trent recoiled as he felt the bone drawing him closer.

Eli placed the bone at the entrance of the room and left the cave, saying, "Enjoy your eternity in this cave, Trent. Everett will die on his own because he will need to eat and drink and without you supplying food, he will die in a week."

"That's why you told me the story? You knew all along that you could escape, why wait until now?"

Trent sat back, unable to move more than three feet in front of him.

"It's simple. I just like to tell the story and I didn't convince young Everett here to replace the bone until recently. He's not the smartest of mortals." Eli tipped his hat and left Everett in a trance-like state, unable to move.

Trent vowed to his wife and his friends to make everything right, but that arm bone prevented him from leaving the small room.

He didn't feel the finality of death yet.

He had a plan that would make everything right, but he couldn't determine how to release himself, and it appeared that Everett would be of no use to him.

***.

A few days had passed, and he saw something dart around the arm. A single bat began eating the rotting flesh, slightly moving the arm.

Soon more bats were present and they feasted on the remnants of his arm. After a few hours, he couldn't see the arm because hundreds of bats eating obscured its view, and moved it farther away from the living and breathing Everett. Everett got weaker but there was no food to toss to him.

"Come on guys, just a few more feet," he uttered, as the bats fought over the few scraps still attached to the bone.

Suddenly, they carried the arm away from the entrance, and Trent felt the power return to him. He escaped and immediately tended to Everett. He removed the trance, and Everett fell face-first onto the hard stone cave floor.

He gathered the five-gallon jug of water and poured it in Everett's mouth. His mouth moved in his unconscious state, sucking up as much as he could. In a flash, Trent left the cave, returned with edible fruit, and stuffed it in his mouth.

Everett awoke, not knowing what had happened to him over the last few weeks.

"Welcome back, Everett!" Trent said, as the weakened man fell back seeing him stand before him.

"Where am I?" he questioned, as he feverishly devoured the rest of the fruit.

"You're in a cave. Do you recall anything in the last few weeks?" Trent asked.

"Yes, I talked with my father." The realization of his situation hit him. "Oh shit! You're going to kill me! Aren't you?"

"No, I'm not going to kill you. In fact, I have to keep you alive at all costs," Trent reassured the shaken man.

Once Everett was confident that Trent wouldn't kill him, Trent explained the whole story to him, and he refused to believe it.

"Are you saying that I'm not supposed to be here? And that my father groomed me to kill people?" he asked, as he ate the last of the berries.

"That's right! Your father, who is now a spirit, wants you dead to fulfill his deal with the devil so he left you here to starve and be eaten by the bats. There's a person who witnessed you killing the pastor and the state police are looking for you. The only way that you can extend your life is to turn yourself in. That way you may be protected from Eli, since he can't kill you directly," Trent explained.

"Did you kill my brothers?"

"Yes, but I killed them out of revenge. I didn't know that is what your father wanted me to do. I killed Morgan, Wyatt, and Ethan but I didn't kill Kerry. He walked into that burning house on his own to save his little brother, you. He thought that in death he could help you by using his last power to protect you. Kerry died to protect you from me," he explained.

"I watched Kerry walk toward the house to get his guns when all of the sudden his legs snapped. The house wasn't on fire. He tried to get his guns.

That's when the house caught fire," Everett disclosed.

"No, maybe that's what Kerry saw and that's what you saw, but the house was completely engulfed and he died instantly." Trent continued. "Let's look at it this way. If you don't turn yourself into the police, I will kill you right here and right now!" Trent didn't declare that he really needed him alive.

“Okay! I’ll turn myself in, can we leave now?” he asked, knowing that he’d rather be in jail alive than dead in the next instant.

Trent was happy that he fell for his bluff. He followed Everett all the way to town where the newly formed police department placed him in handcuffs and locked him up.

Trent didn’t know where Eli was but speculated that he was at the same spot where they’d first met. Trent appeared before him and Eli was dumbfounded as to how he escaped.

Trent confronted him. “All those lies about going to heaven and the next step in the death process was bullshit, wasn’t it?”

“For the most part it was, but I don’t know everything. Where’s Everett?” he asked, as he calmly detached his mule from the cart.

“He’s in jail charged with murder. Eating three square meals a day. I suspect that he’ll live a long life in jail.”

Eli laughed at Trent and imparted, “Do you honestly think him being in jail will stop me from having him killed? It’s already in the works because, as you know, Remy used to be a very beloved man in town, and I suppose that there are at least ten people who’d want to kill him.”

“I knew that you would do that eventually. I can’t stop it, but at least I didn’t kill him.”

"I have news for you, Trent. It just happened! A police officer shot and killed him trying to escape. Everett is dead so I'll be leaving you now. Thanks for making my dream a reality!"

Those were Eli's final words as he disappeared without a trace from the spirit world and back into the mortal realm.

Not knowing what to do, Trent felt that he'd let down everyone who wasn't supposed to be dead, and he sank into a spiritual depression. He was alone in the woods with nothing, but an eternity of loneliness in his future.

Chapter 21
Eli's New Existence

A day later, a very much alive Eli walked out of the woods, went directly to the Tavern, and drank a few beers. It was a pleasure that he'd missed for many years. He was a young man but the people recognized him, although they were amazed that he looked as young as he did. Many in town were skeptical because of his youth since he'd left so long ago, and he should have been pushing seventy, but DNA tests proved that he was who he said he was.

Just as he'd speculated, Randolph's fortune went to him and he moved into his palatial estate and began living the good life.

Trent's spirit was still stuck in the woods with very little hope of righting all the wrongs perpetrated by Eli. He decided that if he weren't able to defeat Eli, then he'd attempt to make his life miserable.

However, Eli was smart. He gathered up the rest of Trent's body, removed all the flesh, and placed multiple bones around his house to prevent Trent from invading his space. Eli's bones were of no use now as they all disappeared when he regained his life.

Trent had nothing to disturb Eli's idyllic life nor could he scare him into thinking that he was being haunted. Trent didn't feel defeated; he still had plenty of time to think of something to reverse the evil that Eli had wrought on so many innocent souls.

Many times, Trent tried to penetrate his fortress but Eli thwarted him each time. He needed to exact revenge but he didn't have a clue as to how. Eli always carried a remnant of Trent's body on his person wherever he went, so Trent couldn't attack him as he walked around town. The perfect Kryptonite to keep him away.

He wondered what Eli meant about going back in time and changing things, but no power he conjured indicated that he even had the ability to do what Eli had done.

If he did, he would never be born and his father would have to die, but if his father did die, everyone else would live the perfect life as told by Eli. Trent didn't know what to do.

Returning to the cave, he saw the two newspaper articles that he took from his father's safe, one that reported his father's death and one that reported that Patch had saved him.

Trent realized that both newspapers were correct and that given Randolph knew where his father's safe was, he concluded that he must have placed them there suppling Trent with a clue.

He looked at the identical photos on the front pages and wondered who took them. The photo pictured the four boys and one girl in the water. However, Patch walked out of the pond.

Something didn't make sense to him because Patch, or Eli, told him that they were fishing, and according to the article, they were swimming. He read the article again but according to the photo, it appeared to be impossible for Glover to throw his father in the pond because Ben was already in the water, well away from the shore. The only way to discern what really happened was to talk to the old man again. However, he was now 108 years old, and Trent thought that if a spirit came to him, it might be too much of a shock.

The last thing he wanted was to drive the man to a heart attack, but he had to talk to him and present him with the old newspapers to ask which one was the correct one.

Trent went to the only person who was still alive and at the scene where his father nearly died.

He appeared at Glover's modest farm, overgrown with weeds due to neglect.

Trent stood nearby as Glover drove his tractor trying to eradicate the weeds.

He saw Glover in the distance driving directly toward him and waited there, to ease the shock of him just appearing in the old man's living room.

Glover saw Trent standing in the fields yet he still drove toward him and stopped a hundred feet away. He climbed off the tractor and walked toward him.

"Hi, ghost! What are you doing in my field?" he asked, wiping his brow.

Trent smiled because the last time Glover called him that, he wasn't, but this time, Glover was correct.

"I've come to ask you a question or two," Trent said, holding out the two newspaper articles.

Glover took a few steps toward him. "Sure, come on up to the house; the sun is too hot out here," he asserted.

"Sure," said Trent as the two walked toward the house.

Trent noted that the centenarian was very spry for his age and walked fast and steady. They arrived at the house a few minutes later and walked inside. Trent placed the articles on the table in front of him. The man picked up the first one, which reported Ben's death, and said that it was the correct one.

"Who took this photo?" Trent asked.

"I took the picture because I needed proof the kids were doing what I told the police and their parents they did. I didn't want them to drown in that old pond."

"Who is the boy you threw in the pond?"

Glover pointed to the boy who came out of the water as the one he threw in.

Trent looked at whom he pointed to and realized that he pointed to Patch, and not his father.

"That's not my father, Ben Pritchard. That's Elijah O'Flaherty. My father is way out here," Trent pointed out on the photo.

The old man scratched his head and asked, "That's not Ben Pritchard?"

Trent assured him that Ben Pritchard was the one way out in the pond whose head was barely poking over the water line.

"This is the boy I tried to save. He's the one that drowned," Glover stated definitively.

"No, that's another boy and he didn't drown. So, the boy that you threw in is not the one who drowned. The boy out there is the one who died," Trent disclosed.

The old man sat the newspaper down and a smile came over his face. It was though Trent lifted a tremendous weight from his soul, but the sad fact that any boy drowned stilled weighed heavy on his heart.

There was another photo presented in both newspapers depicting the other kids running away and Ben still alive and swimming toward the shore. The picture depicted Jordy, Margie, Randolph, and Remy running away as Ben swam, but he didn't see Patch. He looked closer at the second photo, and there he was, hiding under the bank, seemingly waiting for Glover to leave.

Then it all sparked as to what really happened that day. Glover was actually trying to save Patch and when he dived into the water, Patch feigned that he was dead underwater.

When Glover left the scene, Patch held an exhausted Ben underwater until he was dead, then waded out of the water.

Trent was sure that was what happened that day, but he didn't have a reason why Eli had done such a thing. It took only a few minutes of thinking before he answered his own question. Margie, his mother, had a huge crush on Ben back then, and Patch was in love with her. It was actually a crime of passion or a case of deadly puppy love of eleven-year-olds. Regardless, Glover didn't kill his father and, in fact, had killed no one.

"You mean to tell me that had I waited a few minutes more, young Ben would have made it to the shore and not been killed?" Glover asked.

"That's right. Patch killed my father after you left. My father's legs didn't get caught in an underwater branch. One of his best friends killed him because my mother, Margie, liked him more than she liked Patch. It must have been easy for the rested Patch to take my father under the water just long enough to kill him," Trent reiterated.

"But this other newspaper said that he was saved by that same boy you said killed him." Glover pointed to the newer newspaper.

"That's because after his death, a year later, he made a pact with a dark force to return to the scene and change my father's fate so my father would be alive to save him up on the mountain a year later," Trent explained.

"I remember that lost boy on the mountain. They never found him," Glover remembered.

Trent looked at the man and said, "It's amazing that you remember what really happened that day and not the reality that Patch changed. Perhaps people should have believed you."

"I have a question for you, though. If what you say is true and this boy went back in time and altered what happened, how is it that your father didn't tell everyone that Patch, as you call him, tried to drown him?" Glover asked.

"Because when he went back, he didn't try to drown him. He just allowed him to swim as far as he could and helped him get to the shore."

"You spirits can go back and change time?" Glover asked.

"I think I can once, but I wasn't there at the pond that day. Only the people who were there can go back and alter the outcome," Trent further explained. "Oh, and you're right, I am a ghost."

"I knew it! See, I'm not that crazy old man! Son, you have lifted a huge weight off my mind. For over fifty years, I held this burden, but now I know that I didn't kill that kid. I owe you a tremendous debt. Can I ask you a question?" Glover asked, afraid of the answer.

"Sure, Mr. Glover. What do you want to know?"

He folded up the newspaper. "Does it hurt when you die?"

Trent saw that the old man was concerned because he was very old and knew that his time was just about up. "Mr. Glover, no, it doesn't hurt. You are about to go to a beautiful place, but only if you allow it to come when it's your time, so don't get impatient. It will be there for you when fate decides to allow you to see it."

Glover, with tears in his eyes, stated, "It sounds like a beautiful place. I've never been afraid to die but it makes it even easier knowing that there are other steps to climb after I pass. I wish I could have gone back and changed many things in my life. I hope the good Lord will overlook many of those things."

Trent thought about what Glover said, about going back and changing things, and wondered about the possibilities to send a living person back in time to alter what happened. But he was sure that old man Glover wouldn't want to do it if it meant making sure Patch actually killed his father, correcting what Eli had altered. Trent realized the implications, but since he was already dead, he didn't care for himself. He was concerned that he was thinking about going back in time and killing his father, whom he adored growing up.

A sacrifice had to be made to make things right.

It was a paradox that he wished he didn't have to be involved. Trent enjoyed his thirty years of being alive, less the two years after Amanda's death, and had his memories, but realized if he was able to do what Eli pulled off, then everything in his world would immediately cease to exist, including himself.

He also had to sacrifice his spiritual self and his soul, as well as that of his father's, although he suggested to himself that his father was already where he was supposed to be, albeit as an eleven-year-old child who'd never realize adulthood.

Trent, perplexed as he left old man Glover's home, felt happy to have made him realize that he committed no sin so long ago.

Trent appeared at Eli's estate, regardless of the fear of being absorbed into one of the bones sprinkled around his property. He confronted him with what he found out.

Regardless of Eli's new standing in the living world, he was still conscious of the fact that he used to be a spirit and remembered the path he took to get where he is, so he expected visits from Trent.

"I know you're here, Trent! You might as well show yourself," said Eli, as he sat by his pool where two young women frolicked.

"Are you talking to us, Eli?" one of the women asked.

"No, Terri. Why don't you and Ginger go inside and get ready for our trip to Florida next week?" he asked, clearing a way for having a conversation with Trent.

The two bikini-clad women walked out of the pool and entered the house.

Trent appeared. He noticed that Eli still had a hint of a bone decoratively adorned as an ornament around his neck and was sure to stay clear of it. He angrily spoke, "I know what you did by that pond, Eli. Glover is not the one who killed my father, you did!"

Chapter 22
Trent's Ace in the Hole

Eli smiled and calmly stated, "Very good, Trent! You're right. I hated that Margie seemed to like Ben and Randolph, and thought that if I eliminated Ben then she may see me in a different light. Had it been Randolph instead of Ben, I would have done the same thing to eliminate one of my rivals. Very brave of you to come here knowing that one false move could make you disappear for an eternity."

"It was a chance I had to take. I know I can't harm you here but, I will go back and I will make things right!" Trent threatened.

Eli laughed and begged him to try, then said with a smirk on his face, "I told you, Trent. You can't go back because you weren't there at the pond that day. Everyone who was there is dead.

That part of my history is blocked forever and if you can't change that, then you can't change my reality."

Trent smiled right back with an equally devilish smirk and said, "There is one who is still alive and who was there, asshole!"

Eli jerked up with that realization, and wondered what Trent knew and what he was going to do. Still, he didn't know about Mr. Glover and his involvement in the event. He thought back to that time, but he still didn't realize that Glover was the one of whom Trent spoke of. Eli prided himself in covering all his bases, but he saw confidence in Trent's resolve and it scared him.

Then, like a bolt of lightning, he remembered, looked up to Trent's fading spirit and screamed, "Glover! Shit!"

He saw a broad smile on Trent's face as he disappeared, and knew he'd have to place his trip to Florida with his two girlfriends on hold, because he had a murder to commit.

Leery about informing Eli of Glover, he had to get him to make a mistake in his protected and ill-gotten lifestyle. Trent wouldn't allow Eli to kill Glover, and would use all his powers to protect the man from harm.

Immediately appearing at Glover's farm, Trent watched for anything usual; he was thankful that Glover never left his farm since he grew his own food and had everything he needed. He gave him a gift to supply life to his lonely existence.

It was only mere goldfish in a gallon jug, but it was enough to keep the old man's spirits high. He loved the gift and doted over his new colorful friends. Trent was also thankful that Glover was in extraordinarily good health and had many years left.

Five hours later, a dark sedan approached Glover's farm. The farmer didn't see the sedan slowly drive forth, but Trent did and stood directly in its path. The car stopped and four paid assassins with guns drawn were face-to-face with Trent holding his ground in the middle of the long driveway leading to the Glover farm. The men saw Trent but something strange occurred.

They saw through him. They looked at each other and decided to open fire on the image, but it had no effect on Trent as he lifted his hands and raised the car off the ground. Dumbfounded, the men stood completely still. Trent snapped his fingers and the men dropped dead in front of him. He gathered the bodies and placed them back in the car, which was still in midair, and sent the car away in a flash, placing it in Eli's luxurious pool.

It would be up to Eli to get rid of the bodies, discreetly.

***

Eli woke up the next morning to screams when his girlfriend's found the car and the bodies of the four men in the pool when they decided to take a morning dip.

Running out to the pool area, Eli saw the car, and knew that Trent was behind it, and that he was now protecting Glover from harm. In his present form, Eli was powerless against Trent's powers, and had to think of something else to thwart Trent's plans. He also had to get rid of the bodies before he could get a tow truck over to remove the car from his pool. Eli had no powers and had to remove the bodies himself, but it proved difficult because a few of the men were very large.

***

Trent knew that Glover didn't want to relive that tragic time in his life. To change things back to the way fate originally planned, he had to convince Glover to go back and fix everything, but he didn't know what he could say to convince him.

Now, Trent had two goals: to protect Glover from Eli and get Glover to go back and fix things. He erred when he allowed Eli to figure it out, but he also wanted to draw him out with hopes that he'd forget about the trinket around his neck. For history's sake, though, he had to set it right and was willing to sacrifice himself to do it.

Eli planned to have Trent be his own executioner, because he banked on the fact that Trent wouldn't sacrifice his own existence and the rest of his father's life to go back and change what he'd changed. Eli thought that the only recourse for Trent was to give in and enter one of the relics around his property.

***

Daily, Trent made his presence known to Glover, and he began to see that the old man looked forward to seeing the spirit, given that he had no family left with the exception of his goldfish who he talked to with great affection.

Trent was his one and only friend in his day-to-day existence. They played checkers and Trent assisted him in the fields and did all the hard work around the farm that Glover ignored because he was just too old to make it right.

Trent gradually became good friends with the old man. Glover didn't know that he had his own guardian angel looking after him. He felt happy to have someone, or in Trent's case, something, to talk to, who actually talked back to him.

Eli attempted to get to Glover many times over the next month through assassins, and a few times when Eli himself tried to do the deed, but Trent thwarted every potential attack. Eli got worried as he tried to remove the last hurdle to him being safe.

One night, Trent came to Glover to play a game of checkers, and Glover had a health emergency. He fell to the floor right in front of Trent, who called an ambulance.

Glover was still conscious and saw that Trent was with him, so he felt at ease as he held his hand while the ambulance delivered him to the hospital.

Trent was invisible to the medical technicians, but Glover saw him.

He'd had a heart attack, which weakened him, and he called out to his long-deceased wife and his two daughters who died before him, but all he saw was Trent, who promised to not leave his side. Trent had grown very fond of old man Glover, and at times, forgot that he needed him to fix what Eli took.

Glover struggled to speak, "Do you think God will look kindly to me if I fixed what had been altered?"

"I'm sure he will. Fate will be your guide to your family."

Eli got word of Glover's health emergency, sat back, and smiled because he knew that a one hundred-and-eight-year-old man couldn't withstand the life he was living with a bad heart, so it was all a matter of time before he died naturally. He also wondered aloud, "If he has Glover to go back in time and change what I changed, why hasn't he'd done it already?"

He was sure that Trent hadn't found out how to accomplish that. He also concluded that Glover didn't want to relive that time, and he was correct. He decided to just sit back and wait for him to die.

***

At the hospital, it didn't look good for Glover. He died many times during his recovery process but the doctors always brought him back. Trent had no power to save him should death take him, and one day it did.

Glover was in the hospital for three weeks before the end came. Trent was there to ease his passing with words of encouragement. He reminded him of his wife and kids who'd see him again soon.

Just as he said that, Eli walked in the hospital room and saw Trent hovering over the old man.

"You lose, Trent! Unless you have someone who was hiding in the weeds back then," Eli speculated.

"No, I don't but I'm not worried in the least," Trent said, with a huge smile on his face.

"You lost. Admit it! What have you got to smile about?" he asked.

Trent started to fade away as he explained, "I'm not worried because Glover and I had a long talk prior to him dying. For the first time since that event happened, he felt free because he realized that he didn't kill anyone but felt remorse knowing that he'd wasted all those years thinking that he was a murderer, so I gave him an opportunity to go back and make things the way they were prior to him dying here."

"Bullshit! Trent, I know Glover's religious beliefs. He wouldn't allow your father to be killed even by me," he stated definitively.

"Are you sure, Eli? Imagining a lifetime free of guilt could change any man's thoughts. He knew that you were evil for killing your friend. He is all for striking evil when it comes to him. He also knew that he was ready to die here but felt sorry that he'd wasted all those years. I merely gave him an opportunity to relive his life free of that guilt. He immediately overrode your changes just by the fact that he went back there and will allow you to kill my father."

"If he does that then you'll cease to exist."

"That's right. I forfeited my existence to make things right. Memories of me will no longer linger within people's minds. My father's friends will be alive, my mother will be alive, Amanda will be alive, as well as your parents and your sisters.

However, you will die all over again in the mouths of wolves in that field you told me about. I will visit that site with the last essence of my being and laugh as they drag your sorry body away and remove every hint of your existence as well."

"That's not possible! I'm still here and you're fading. I'm assuming that your father is losing his battle with the pond. When you disappear completely, your father will be dead. I realize that I will be as well, but I'll attempt another prophecy as I did before and start the whole process again," he stated with a smile.

"No, you see, you made a mistake by killing Kerry the way you did. You made it seem to him that the house was not on fire as he crawled toward it. You used your powers to kill Kerry, so I doubt that the prophecy will be there for you again. You see, I've been learning. I may be gone before you but I have the pleasure of knowing that you are right behind me," Trent stated.

Eli countered, "However, you've forgotten that even if I can't come back to life, I will be able to endure in the spiritual world, whereby you, having never been born, will never know that."

Trent's image faded further.

Eli also faded from view and quickly disappeared from the hospital room, but something strange happened when his spirit disappeared.

***

Trent awoke in a plush bed with satin sheets in a spacious room full of expensive antiques. He sat up and wondered where he was, and who he was. He ran to the mirror to see that he looked exactly the same. He pinched himself and felt pain.

He was alive but didn't know why. Someone shouted in his direction.

"Isaac," the woman called.

Trent said nothing until he saw the woman walk into the room. "Mom! Is it really you?"

It was his mother Margie, and she begged him to hurry, "Of course it's me. Whom else were you expecting? You're going to have to get up out of that bed and get ready. Remember, you're getting married today?"

Trent was thankful to see his mother as happy as she was.

"Come on! Your father is almost ready and we don't want to be late."

She brought out his tuxedo and placed it on the bed. "Hurry, dear; take a shower already! Do you want to be late to your own wedding?"

"My wedding?" he asked himself. "I'm not even supposed to be here and I'm getting married?"

Still shaking his head, he walked toward the open bathroom door.

Another person walked in the room imploring him to hurry. It was Randolph Kolb, and he was apparently married to his mother, so he was now a Kolb himself.

He wondered if somehow this was heaven because he saw all the people he once thought dead.

He'd had a long, sustained dream about death, spirits, revenge, and wondered how true it all was and if his existence was the result of his father dying sixty years prior, or an elaborate and visually vivid dream.

He remembered that his name was Isaac Kolb; he remembered the high school and college he attended; and that he was the son of a United States Senator.

Showered and dressed, his new father moved him along so fast that he didn't even think about whom he was marrying. He was so happy to see his mother happy, and Randolph introduced him to his two bubbly sisters on the way to the church.

According to his mother, he was incredibly late and there was little time for questions or breathing for that matter. He and Randolph Kolb walked toward the flower-wrapped arch as the *Wedding March* played.

Then he saw his betrothed. Amanda walked down the aisle with Pastor Remy firmly holding her arm. Isaac stared at her as she cried and discreetly welcomed guests and wiped her eyes all the way.

She arrived at the altar to hold both of Isaac's hands. He harkened back to his dream, and wondered why he was there if Ben died at that pond at eleven years old. Then a possible answer came to him. Since he looked exactly the same, was it possible that he had always been the son of Randolph Kolb? he wondered.

Even in his dream, Randolph Kolb was dating his mother prior to his father and mother marrying.

Suppose his mother was pregnant with Kolb's baby when they married? He further wondered.

He needed to concentrate on his wedding and get his dream out of his mind, but then speculated if it had really happened. Then all the pieces fell into place.

"What's wrong, Isaac? Your mind seems to be elsewhere." Amanda moved a stray hair from her face.

"I'm sorry, I just can't get over how beautiful you are. I can't wait to start our time together." He gently kissed her.

The pastor, seeing them kiss before they said their vows, asked, "Do you guys want to get married or should I come back later?"

"Oops, sorry, Daddy! We're ready!" she said, as she looked to her father, but she couldn't help herself and turned toward Isaac to watch his reaction to what was happening.

They said their vows, kissed, then ran down the aisle to the cheers of all who were present and throwing flower petals to the newlyweds all the way to the car.

Isaac still wondered about all that had happened that day, but he was extremely happy and decided that he'd no longer care about the dream and would live his life to the fullest.

***

A year went by and Isaac and Amanda welcomed their first child.

The happy couple named him Benjamin after a long-lost friend of his father's, Benjamin Pritchard, who died as a child in Glover's pond.

The Knolls called to the couple and they climbed the small hill to see a scene that Isaac had seen before in that vivid dream that he still thought about often.

It seemed strange that everything he had dreamed seemed to be coming to him, right down to Amanda's silhouetted body through her white dress and the bears in the distance at the tree line.

One very noticeable omission from the dream was the Kolb brothers and their reign of terror over the town, was non-existent.

Red Dirt officially had its name. State Senator Randolph Kolb created it and gave the town fifty acres surrounding it. He and his wife created opportunities for everyone in town, but it was Isaac's vision that created the town's look.

He opened a tavern, and called it Balls Bluff and hired a young woman named Nancy to run it with the promise that she'd eventually own it.

The townspeople flocked to Remy's church and he preached to a full house every Sunday.

The need for a Sportsmen store cropped up because hunting and fishing were still the favorite pastime of the residents.

He fashioned the town based on his dream, and he was certainly happier in real life than in his amazingly vivid dream.

He was on a hunting trip when his dream confronted him again. He and his dog were dove hunting in a field that he hadn't stepped foot on since his childhood.

As his dog ran through the high grass, four doves flew off. Isaac aimed and fired but missed the birds as a voice rang out.

"Nice try. Perhaps your sights need to be adjusted," an old man sitting on a nearby rock, said.

"Where did you come from, mister?" Isaac asked.

"Oh, I've been around here for years. How did you do it, Trent? How were you able to come back?" he asked, to the astonishment of Isaac.

"Trent? My name is Isaac Kolb. Who are you?" he asked, wary of seeing the old man in the middle of nowhere.

The leather-clothed man asked, "You don't recognize me, do you?"

"No! Should I know you?"

"I'm Elijah O'Flaherty. I am a friend of your father when we were kids. He called me Patch."

"Patch? Oh, shit! It isn't real! I dreamed of a man named Patch. It was a horrible nightmare!" he declared, excitedly.

Eli jumped off the rock, walked toward Isaac, and stated, "It's no nightmare. It's as real as you and me standing here." He muted his barking dog with a wave of his hand.

Isaac raised his gun as he stepped backward and called his dog.

Eli smiled and said, "A gun? Are you serious, Trent?" He raised his hand again and concentrated on the barrel and it began to get hot. So hot that it eventually glowed red.

Isaac threw it aside, grabbed his knife, and held it in front of him. “It was just a fucking dream! You don’t exist!” he explained, as he stepped back.

“Trent, I want to know how you were able to come back as Isaac. You look exactly the same! Your father died, and I died right over there, and now I’m stuck here and you were able to return to life,” he explained.

“I don’t know what you’re talking about. Now back away!” Isaac warned.

“You know exactly what I’m talking about! The Kolb brothers are my sons, the prophecies, the death and mayhem that you and I caused, and your final act that ousted me from the very house you and your pretty wife are living in. The first time, I allowed you to do what you wanted but now, I’m just pissed!” Eli stated, as he walked closer to Isaac.

“I am Isaac Kolb and I’ve always been Isaac Kolb. I have no brothers but I will not step back any farther. What do you want from me?” he asked, as he stopped walking backward.

“I want what you have. I want to live. You say that you don’t know what the prophecy is. Well, I’m going to revise it and I will sacrifice you, your parents, and even your son to realize that end. There is nothing you can do about it, Trent.”

The spirit picked up Isaac and threw him fifty feet away. Trent landed on soft, high grass that broke his fall.

Eli saw Isaac's floppy hat knocked off because of his attack, and placed it on his head as he walked slowly toward the fallen and shaken man.

"Did that hurt, Trent? Tell me something: what did old man Glover have to give up to go back. He didn't have five most dear."

Isaac reverted back to his dream and said, "Goldfish! Five goldfish. He loved those fish."

Eli chuckled at the barking dog and wanted to blow it up but he couldn't attack the dog and he didn't know why.

"What's going on? Get the hell away from me!"

He felt the dog's teeth burrowing through his skin.

"How is this happening? What the fuck is happening to me? Are you doing this, Trent?" Eli saw something eating his legs away. He removed Isaac's hat. "Where did you get this hat?"

Isaac, seeing that something affected the spirit, pointed to a lone tree in the meadow.

"But that's where I died and the wolves ate my carcass there… This is my fucking hat!" he realized as he folded down the band to reveal the initials EO. "Shit! Some of my hairs are still in this hat. Hairs that were there when I died."

He fell to his knees and looked at Trent. "I guess you didn't need my bones to kill me. A single fucking hair?"

In a whisk of a breeze, Eli turned black and what was left of him blew toward the tree, destroying any hope of going back and destroying Isaac's life.

Isaac said, "I guess I win! Eh, Eli?" He picked up the hat, walked over to the tree, and saw the rest of a child's remains. It was just bones but Isaac knew that they were just bones from an asshole he'd dreamed of; nothing more, nothing less.

He threw his hat on the skeleton and said, "I hope that you enjoy hell, you son of a bitch! I got my wife and child back and I got my life back and all you got is a stained old hat and a death completely devoid of a next step."

Isaac gathered up his dog and his rifle, grabbed a stick, and threw it far in front of him. His dog took off through the tall grass, grabbed it, and brought it back.

He looked back to the tree in the middle of the meadow, smiled, and said, "Let's go home, boy! We have people who love us there and are waiting for our return. There's nothing here but grass and one very dead asshole devoid of spirit and soul."

The End